BAKER'S DOZEN

First published 2023

Copyright © Vida Cody 2023

The right of Vida Cody to be identified as the author of this work has been asserted in accordance with the Copyright, Designs & Patents Act 1988.

All rights reserved. No part of this book may be reproduced, stored in a retrieval system, or transmitted in any form or by any means, digital, electronic, electrostatic, magnetic tape, mechanical, photocopying, recording or otherwise, without the written permission of the copyright holder.

This is a work of fiction. Any similarity to actual persons, living or dead, or actual events, is purely coincidental and not intended by the author.

Published under licence by Brown Dog Books and
The Self-Publishing Partnership Ltd, 10b Greenway Farm, Bath Rd, Wick, nr.
Bath BS30 5RL, UK

www.selfpublishingpartnership.co.uk

ISBN printed book: 978-1-83952-728-9
ISBN e-book: 978-1-83952-729-6

Cover design by Andrew Prescott
Internal design by Andrew Easton

Printed and bound in the UK

This book is printed on FSC® certified paper

BAKER'S DOZEN
Tales from a country village

VIDA CODY

For Tia
With love

CONTENTS

1	Andrew's Story	11
2	Lydia and Mr Wickham	16
3	The Freebies	23
4	Kathleen	31
5	Thelma	38
6	Miss Scarlet	44
7	Cerberus	52
8	The Village Post	59
9	The Outsider	67
10	Mr and Mrs Prima Donna	76
11	Brown Bread	83
12	The Clocks	90
13	The Man Who Married the Vicar	99
14	Unquiet Slumbers	107

CAST OF CHARACTERS IN LITTLE BUNTING

1. Andrew, the baker
2. Annie and Jimmy, the re-enactors
3. The Freebies, out for what they can get, and their daughter, Mary Sue
4. Kathleen, former chef
5. Thelma, former art teacher and headmistress
6. Ruby, the village vixen, aka Miss Scarlet
7. Cerberus, the Yorkie and Bob, his master
8. Ted and Jean, the postman and his wife
9. Faisal, the poet
10. Ken the builder and his wife Darlene, a former Hollywood actress
11. Gabriella, the dying woman
12. Lottie, the single mum
13. The vicar of St Luke's and husband Matthew
14. Ginny, senior historian and archivist

SUPPORTING CHARACTERS
Four fine Percherons
Major Morton
Some tired Spanish waiters
Lottie's mum and daughters Meg and Chloé
Chester the cat
Bailey the Basset Hound
Various ghosts

ANDREW'S STORY

Andrew Baker was just that. A baker. It was by good fortune alone that his name matched his profession, 'though he might have changed it anyway if it hadn't. It was one of those names of old that he'd inherited, that described a man's vocation, like Mason, Taylor and Fletcher. He'd liked to have been Mr Bun, like the Happy Families character, but Baker did just as well. It said what it was on the tin and drew people in for the novelty value alone.

Andrew was always the practical type who could turn his hand to anything, be it carpentry, bricklaying, baking or sewing. His house in the country was testament to this, on the inside as well as out, admired by all who saw it for its cosy cottage charm and tasteful home furnishings. He had come to Little Bunting just two years ago, having relocated from his native Scotland after losing his job at the local distillery to a younger and less experienced man. It was the way of the world these days and Andrew just had to get on with it.

After a few searches online, he'd found a good-sized plot of land for sale, on the edge of the pretty little village that would soon become his home for good. Within a few months, the foundations were laid and, little by little, the house emerged, in honey coloured Cotswold stone, overlooking a pleasant valley.

Andrew liked to entertain and many a night had seen a gathering, out on the patio when the evenings were warm, listening to the song of a nightingale. Andrew himself was a nature lover, having spent a good deal of his childhood sitting in hides on the Scottish estates, watching and waiting patiently. His parents had taught him to sit quite still and to keep his voice as low as he could if he wanted the wildlife to come before him. His reward had been a variety of beasts, from red deer and otters to eagles and ospreys.

His father and mother had both worked in oil, having moved up north from their London home when promotion within the company called. George had been a sub-sea engineer, designing and installing underwater equipment while Barbara had worked in senior management as part of a vital onshore team. Not long after they'd left the south, little Andrew came to be born. He grew up proud of his English roots while adopting Scotland as his primary home, his love for the country all consuming.

His parents had died when Andrew was young, before he'd taken his Higher Exams. Their car had crashed on an icy road as they journeyed together to work one day. The teenage Andrew became an orphan with no parents and no siblings but inherited a house and a good deal of money, the latter kept in a fund till eighteen.

Baker's Dozen

He'd graduated from Heriot-Watt with a first-class degree in Brewing and Distilling before taking a job at a distillery, learning his trade as an expert stillman, responsible for the production process and maintaining the iconic copper stills. He loved his job in the industry, enthusing colleagues and customers alike with his unique blend of artistry and charming, easy-going manner.

After thirty years, he was glad of the change, to try his hand at something new, having faced down the barrel of redundancy. He decided he'd like to work for himself, to change direction, toil fewer hours. Andrew surprised many of his friends when he left his home and moved away, itchy feet taking him south. Some had called it a mid-life crisis but Andrew had lost none of his confidence and showed no sign of troubling thoughts.

He'd arrived in the village in his sporty car, a bright red Morgan with a running board, turning many a female head. It soon became known that Andrew was single with every possible manly attribute. He wasn't particularly looking for a wife ('though many, it seemed, were looking for him) but his eyes were open all the same, in this new and exciting world he was in.

He rented a shop in the nearby town – to his amusement, formerly Capon's the butcher, old man Capon having retired and his sons not inclined to handle meat. He turned it into a bakery, from where he'd supply the local town and his own, new, village community.

Baker's Dozen

He catered for every type of taste, from white and brown to focaccia and sourdough, from black bread that was good for the gut to crumpets, croissants and breakfast rolls. He readily made bread to order, for special occasions or weekly whims, like naan or pumpernickel, challah, brioche and panettone. His favourite to make was bannock bread as it brought back memories of his Scottish home.

Andrew had a feel for the dough and found the kneading therapeutic. The smell of golden, crusty bread was enough to draw his customers in and those who had their bread delivered waited with their butter knives, hoping that it would still be hot. The Baker's Dozen, he liked to call them, the villagers he delivered to. Popular from the moment he came, Andrew greeted them with a smile, with his soft, soothing, Edinburgh lilt, his sense of humour and gentle ways.

He always delivered by breakfast time as some of the Dozen relied on this, then travelled back to his shop in town, to open for early morning custom. He enjoyed his early bakery round, a quick chat at every house, with a promise to come the following day to those who liked their croissants fresh.

The Baker's Dozen were a varied group, some quite young, others old. They ranged in personality, from retiring types and the modestly clever to the nosy parkers and the mildly eccentric, with every trait in between. A mix of elements, like his bread – crusty, coarse, soft and sweet, tender, rough, fluffy and airy – the ingredients of many an English village. Their differences made the world go round; it would be boring if they were all the same and Andrew delighted in every one, with one or two wearisome exceptions.

In their turn, they all loved him, for his bread, his character and his sheer good looks. Tall and muscular with a broad chest and strong arms and a relaxed but confident walk, Andrew was popular in the community, not least to a legion of adoring women. The female vicar would see him married if any way could be arranged. She'd even consider him herself if she hadn't been wed to a hunk already.

Andrew took it all in his stride and thought it a harmless bit of fun. He'd always enjoyed company and hearing what others had to say, accepting the invites that came his way with an eager pleasure and anticipation. He loved to dine at the vicarage where a warm welcome was always assured and the conversation easily flowed. It was there that he'd first met some of his neighbours, at a sumptuous dinner to welcome him. "Breaking bread" the vicar had said and he'd laughed at her wit and sense of humour. 'Though not a particularly religious man, he knew he'd found his spiritual home for the warm reception he'd been given there and the sense of belonging he immediately felt. His newfound friends were exceptionally kind and he knew how well he had fitted in.

Andrew Baker was like his dough. He could only really rise from here.

LYDIA AND MR WICKHAM

Andrew had first known them as Victoria and Albert – the young couple in the village, recently married and plainly in love, as all newlyweds are. He'd knocked on their door on his morning round, only to have it opened by a diminutive figure dressed in black and looking sad.

She startled him at first with her downcast eyes and mourning clothes, till she raised her head and let out a laugh, clearly delighted at the reaction she'd caused. He'd assumed she was off to a funeral, dressed as she was in her widow's weeds, and wondered if she'd lost her nearest and dearest.

Nothing was further from the truth, as her handsome husband came up behind her and joined her in laughing at Andrew's face, so completely taken in was he by her sombre garb and sepulchral stance. He stood there with his loaf of bread, open-mouthed and completely speechless, clearly shocked and in a daze.

After the couple had stopped laughing, they announced themselves as Annie and Jimmy, the couple who ordered their bread online in contrast to the older folk in the village.

Baker's Dozen

The two were off to a re-enactment, Annie dressed as Queen Victoria, the grief-stricken wife of the young Prince Consort. As Albert himself had already died, Jimmy was forced to go in mufti, 'though sporting the trademark whiskers and moustache as a nod to the man the Queen had lost.

While Andrew thought them a good-looking couple, he was somewhat bemused at their state of dress. He'd never been one for dressing up and preferred to live in the present day, while quietly admiring the courage they'd need to board a train to London that day. He'd love to see the commuters' reaction as they squashed in tight on their way to work, alongside a tiny Queen. It was almost tempting to board himself, to see if anyone spoke or smirked or pretended not to notice them, burying heads in books or phones or even simulating sleep. It was an odd place, the commuter train, and needed a bit of shaking up.

The couple had been to school together and were childhood sweethearts from an early age. Growing up they were never apart, from when they first met as toddlers to their eager and mawkish teenage years. Everyone knew their friendship would last as the two were always there for each other, standing by through thick and thin, rarely leaving the other's side. They'd both gone on to take a degree, Annie in history, Jimmy in art, each with a passion for their discipline and an ever-deepening love for each other. They married after their Final Exams and settled back in Little Bunting, in the house where Jimmy's parents had lived.

Annie was only five feet tall with dark hair and a face like an angel. As a child she'd always been cherubic with chubby cheeks and a little dimple but had lost her roundness when still quite young and was now of slender, sylph-like proportions. Jimmy was tall at six feet two, with a straight back and a military stance. He looked the part at his fencing class, performing his moves with precision and accuracy, in his white breeches and long-sleeved jacket. Annie would go to watch him fence, as he thrust with his foil at lightning speed, his face a picture of concentration. How dashing he'd be in a uniform, 'though she wouldn't want him to go to war.

The perfect solution presented itself in the annual Jane Austen Festival in Bath. Annie and Jimmy loved dressing up and had done so fairly regularly while studying at university. Members of two societies – amateur dramatics and re-enactment – opportunities often came their way to don the costume of someone else. They'd starred in Agatha Christie plays – Jimmy as Poirot, Annie the victim – and numerous works by Noël Coward. Annie had received critical acclaim for acting the part of Madame Arcati, the eccentric medium in *Blithe Spirit*, throwing herself into the role and attracting publicity in the local rag.

Historical events and re-enactments were particularly where they liked to be and they'd often been seen

Baker's Dozen

heading off as Tudor royals in their finery or Elizabethan adventurers.

The Jane Austen Festival was right up their street, as both loved the works of this fine English novelist and the costumes of the era in which she lived. They'd been to her house several times, in the pretty Hampshire village called Chawton – often during Regency Week – attending talks, walks and workshops and immersing themselves in everything Austen, but they hadn't yet been to the Bath parade or to a ball as one of their favourite characters. This happy year was to change all that, as Annie and Jimmy started a plan.

Bath was a city they both knew well, as it wasn't far from their village home. They visited several times a year, to walk in the steps of their heroine and go to the famous Assembly Rooms, the hub of fashionable Georgian society and venue for many an elegant ball.

They walked hand in hand down Milsom Street, through New Bond Street to Pulteney Bridge and further afield to Sydney Gardens. They pictured themselves in a barouche box, arriving in style and magnificent splendour rather than in their jeans and trainers, on foot and coffee in hand. They imagined Miss Austen walking out, looking in windows of milliners' shops, for a new bonnet of cambric muslin or a length or two of white satin trimming. How lovely too she must have looked, when going out for her evening walk, in her kerseymere spencer to keep her warm.

Baker's Dozen

Oh that they could turn back the clock, to see her figure walking there, to hear her voice and her conversation. Or to see her dance in the Upper Rooms, in her neatness of dress and simple slippers.

Annie and Jimmy would need to consider which costumes to wear for the Festival and the fictional characters they intended to be. After hours of laughter and much discussion, they settled on Lydia and Mr Wickham, the foolish and headstrong Bennet girl and the charismatic but deceitful rake.

Two types of garment were needed for both, one for the Festival promenade and one for the elegant evening ball. Annie could easily have made their clothes or, easier still, have hired them in, but the couple chose to purchase them all from a pop-up shop within the town, with the express intent of regular use.

The two arrived for the costumed parade, dressed top to toe in Regency style. Jimmy, as always, looked very becoming, his tall slender frame attracting the girls in his long brown coat, short light waistcoat, figure-hugging breeches and riding boots. Sitting high upon his head, his hat made him look even taller still and he swept it off intermittently with a courteous bow to his pretty wife.

Annie was all simplicity, in her soft, plain pelisse in an earthy brown, over a modest gown with basic adornment. Her bonnet was of a lighter hue, with ruffles all around the edge and a darker ribbon that tied at the neck.

Baker's Dozen

They strolled together, amidst the crowds of bonnets and men in uniform, of exposed bosoms and tight breeches, from the Holburne Museum by Sydney Gardens to the townhouses of the Royal Crescent. Each in their turn drew admiring looks, Annie for her undoubted beauty and Jimmy for his over-confident swagger.

Later that week, in The Paragon, they attended a workshop on Regency dance, learning the steps of the country dances and the elaborate footwork of the cotillions. They needed to put the hours in, rehearse, rehearse, rehearse again, if they were ever to join a set at the ball and line up with countless other couples.

By and by the ball came round, held in the historic Guildhall in Bath. Lydia Bennet and Mr Wickham lent much distinction to the grand assembly as they entered together, arm in arm, their charm exuding from every pore. Passing by the tables for whist and the food laid out in a pleasing arrangement, they walked through the hot and crowded room to take their place for the first dance.

Lyddie was in her empire-line dress, fitted tightly under the bust to emphasise her swelling bosom that threatened to tease the topaz cross that she wore around her swan-like neck. Lightly embroidered in gold thread with a delicate cream flower motif, her long flowing skirt breezed the floor, as the toes of her slippers peeped out beneath. Eschewing a bonnet, she had chosen instead a ringlet of pearls that encircled her bun, drawn up on the top of her head and giving a simple and homely look.

Beside her stood Wickham in military red, the seductive officer who stole every heart. The gold brocade on his epaulettes continued down across his chest in stripes descending as far as his waist. From there, every eye was turned to his breeches with their frontal flap held up with buttons, revealing the shape of his manhood enclosed. Many a heart was sent aflutter as he softly padded about the room in his flat shoes with their fancy buckles.

The two took their place in the first formation, joined by partners from across the floor, weaving in and out in patterns and progressing up and down the set. Their many hours of rehearsal paid off as they never missed a step or cue, standing out as the favoured couple, fitting the sense of occasion perfectly. The Boulanger tested them out as they joined hands and moved in a circle, taking their turn in the middle of the group as the music quickened and their partners changed.

As the evening turned into morning, the music began for the final dance – a stately piece with a number of couples in long lines the length of the room. It was a perfect way to end the ball and round off a whirl of festivities. Lydia and Wickham changed their clothes and Annie and Jimmy reappeared. No carriage waited outside, no horses champing at the bit, just the red car of Andrew the baker, ready to take a tired pair home.

THE FREEBIES

The house on the corner was the one that Andrew had misgivings over. The daughter, Mary Sue, was pleasant enough – hardworking, intelligent and always willing to have a chat whenever they met in town. It was her parents he found tiresome.

Every week it was the same old story when he called to deliver the bread. They took their loaf quickly enough, snatched it even, but never had the money to pay. They hadn't collected their pension that week and had spent what little they had on half a dozen eggs from the local farm and a pint or two of milk. They had to be careful and watch their pennies in these difficult and uncertain times. Could they pay him twice next week when he called again with their loaf? Every time the same conversation, every time he left empty handed, agreeing to add the cost to their slate which by now had reached epic proportions.

He was certain that Mary Sue knew nothing, as he felt her to be an honest type and would never have allowed him to go unpaid. He wondered whether to mention it next time he saw her in the café in town but he didn't want to

Baker's Dozen

embarrass her, especially in such a public space. He'd have to find some other means of extracting the dough from this parsimonious house, perhaps without Mary Sue ever knowing.

Had he known this couple to be really poor or if the age-old narrative was not so frequent, he would willingly have baked them a loaf of bread and would probably have gone the extra mile in bringing them cakes from time to time; but the two were known throughout the village as deceitful, cunning individuals, determined to get their provisions for nothing while assuming an air of abject poverty. They even dressed to look the part, in faded and shabby worn-out clothes, as if it was all they had for their backs when the reality, he knew, was rather different.

They hadn't been in the village long and many hoped that they wouldn't stay. They had gained a notoriety, an unfortunate one and for all the wrong reasons, largely built on their penny-pinching ways. They were known as Mr and Mrs Freeby, the couple who lived at 38. It wasn't their real name of course. It could have been the Robinsons, the Williams or anything else really but Mr and Mrs Freeby is how they were known. Or the Freebies, to those who knew them well. They didn't know that's what they were called and had never ever heard it said but Mr and Mrs Freeby was how everyone referred to them. Or the Freebies, as previously mentioned.

They lived with their daughter, Mary Sue, a kind and

caring fifty-something, who travelled to London every day then returned home to be with her parents. She knew about the Freebies but she wasn't one herself and never planned to be one with their cheapskate reputation. She found it too embarrassing when she heard what neighbours said – that her parents paid for nothing ('though that wasn't strictly true).

They were never very popular down at their local pub as they never bought a round or even a bag of crisps. The two would stand there watching till a friend was at the bar, then quietly sidle over and perform their usual act. It was by now a well-rehearsed routine, as they tried to look hesitant, deciding what to have, then acted all surprised when someone offered a drink. Friends fell for it every time, largely being embarrassed not to, but cursed themselves later for not holding back and waiting to see what happened. Those moments could seem like hours though, as they all stood at the bar, and it was easier to buy a round than stand in anguish waiting, for the Freebies would never offer – of that they could all be certain. The publican called them "Tired Hands" as they never seemed to move – not in their pockets for cash 'though they were quick to pick up a glass.

It wasn't that they were poor. Maybe that was why – because they kept their money to themselves and never spent a penny. Or that was how it seemed as they went to some extremes, like always going to funerals to be sure of

Baker's Dozen

a free meal afterwards. They sang in fine voice at any of the chosen hymns, looked dutifully sad and always wore black. It was wondered by most how they knew so many people, to be always at the grave, always in mourning clothes, but the Freebies carried on without ever seeming to care as long as they went to the reception after and enjoyed a drink and some tasty, catered food.

They had money, of course they did, but were never keen to spend it, going out of their way to avoid paying for anything.

Members of the National Trust, courtesy of Mary Sue, who bought their subscription every year, they certainly made the most of it, going to their local sites several times a month because they knew they could enter for free. It wasn't the houses they were interested in, or even particularly the gardens, but they enjoyed the clean toilets and the nicely smelling soap. They could stay in the café all day, without anyone hurrying them on, nursing the one cup of coffee that they purchased with a voucher. What the Freebies really liked was the free tap water, available all day long and to which they could help themselves. There was no embarrassment here, in going for the umpteenth glass, as they didn't have to ask for it and could just serve themselves.

The water was a puzzle to Mary Sue, as her parents didn't like the taste. They were never considered the healthy type and never drank water at home, unless in a

Baker's Dozen

glass of whisky. It was simply there to be taken, like the white serviettes and the various sachets, all so appealing in their nice, bright colours. Why they should want a sachet of vinegar or mayonnaise with their glass of water was known by all but challenged by none. The Freebies would load them into their bags without so much as a by your leave and nobody said a word.

It was very typical of the couple to take things that weren't even wanted, like cereal bars handed out at the station and other sundry promotional offers. As long as they never had to pay, they took what was offered and went on their way. Some of these "gifts" were later recycled, given away with *grande largesse* as if bestowing a crock of gold, while in reality clearing a cupboard.

The Freebies made an art of it all, doing the rounds of producers' markets, looking for free samples of food to avoid going home and making lunch and basically taking anything going, whether wanted, needed or not. Mary Sue despaired of them both as she wasn't, herself, like this at all. It wasn't that her parents were poor (and God knows she paid for a lot of what they had from her own small pockets), but they did insist on doing everything on the cheap – or for free if they could possibly manage it.

How embarrassed she felt, to see them at the food market, sampling all the food with no intention of buying. There was no cheese left on that stall after her parents had visited. Oh, how embarrassing. Thank God she was over

Baker's Dozen

the other side. No one would know she was with them, let alone related!

They always took the breakfast rolls when staying at some nice, swanky hotel, paid for with Mary Sue's hard-earned cash, and not just the rolls but the fillings too, from cold meat and eggs to tomatoes and cheese. If they were allowed to eat it at breakfast time, they saw nothing wrong with scoffing it for lunch. Mary Sue had paid for it after all.

Like the packets of coffee, sugar and tea in their hotel room, along with those little cartons of milk – UHT but free of charge, which they had replenished whenever they could, in order to build a proper supply to be taken home at the end of the week. They were only pleased to have cancelled the milkman.

And let's not forget the toiletries! All of those wonderful miniatures, the delight of any hotel stay, often arranged in a little basket, with dental floss and shower caps. Mrs Freeby had hundreds of those, 'though she never remembered using any. Why would she want a shower cap when trying out the new conditioner? Where indeed would she put them all, for the bathroom cabinet wasn't that big and there was no room left on the otherwise adequate shelf. Mrs Freeby had taken a box, unwanted at her local grocery store, and into this she had piled her bottles, her night-time creams and shower caps. The dental floss could barely fit, to the extent that she'd had to remove the cases, which gave more room for the floss itself, 'though it often got lost amidst the debris, the flotsam and jetsam of her toiletry stash.

Much was a mystery to Mary Sue, 'though she wondered if it wasn't an age thing. Her parents seemed to horde this stuff while she was one for minimalism. You could barely move in any of their rooms, could scarcely walk across the floor without climbing over a mountain of stuff. It was suffocating, like Tutankhamun's tomb, with objects crammed in everywhere and no sense of a plan or any comfort. Mary Sue was different again, her only room a sanctuary, to which she retreated whenever she could.

Most of the time she accepted their ways, accepted them for who they were, but sometimes it would get her down as she heard the comments around the village, knew what their reputation was. Did they really save that much, by collecting vouchers and abstemious means, or were they just sensibly thrifty? For who wouldn't accept a free gift if lucky enough to be offered one? Such niceties rarely came her way and she began to think she might be jealous. She'd scrimped and saved throughout her life, putting aside what money she could from her less-than-well-paid office job. Most of her friends were happily married and shared any costs with their other half but that had not been Mary Sue's lot, eventually moving in back home when Michael had left for another woman and she couldn't afford a place of her own.

Her retirement years were looming now and Mary Sue looked forward to those. She could say goodbye to the daily commute and the tedious office politics. She could say hello to more free time, to seniors' rates at the cinema and charitable outings from the local church.

Mary Sue sat at the bus stop, waiting impatiently for the number 19 and checking she'd brought her debit card with her. She had no idea what her journey would cost as it all went through on contactless. Either way, she would have to pay, as her monthly statement testified. Mary Sue stopped, as she caught herself thinking of her wonderful, carefree life ahead, her future (free!) seniors' pass and the untold freebies that would come her way. She was one of the family after all.

KATHLEEN

They weren't all like The Freebies, Andrew mused. Most people in the village were lovely and Kathleen was certainly one of them. Elderly now but still one of the girls – in spirit at least, as her body had begun to give up on her. She'd been something of a cracker in her younger days – if the photos were anything to go by – and there was still very much a sparkle in her clear blue eyes and a warmth in her voice whenever she spoke. Nothing and no one would get Kathleen down, 'though much and many had had a good try. She just wasn't the sort. Never had been. She wasn't a glass half full; she was always overflowing. If only there were more like her. What a happy place the world would be. Just like the village (mainly).

In many ways, Kathleen was the soul of the village. The beating heart. It would be a very sad place without her, as one day it would inevitably be, but not today thought Andrew as he delivered her bread and morning croissant. He knew how much she loved those croissants, especially once she'd added some butter. High cholesterol could bide its time as long as she didn't go over the top. No one should

Baker's Dozen

live without their daily pleasures and a buttered croissant hit the spot. What a lovely woman she was, thought Andrew, full of life and happiness. If only she were young again. He'd snap her up no bother.

Kathleen lived on her own now, 'though she'd had a string of men in her time and at least two marriages behind her. She'd begun to lose count. No children had come her way, as she hadn't really wanted any. Too busy enjoying life to be tied to a round of dirty nappies, school runs and swimming galas. It would be nice to have their company now, to share a croissant and a cup of tea, but the village kids would be in later, sharing their tales and making her laugh. The older ones came for advice, usually about their latest crush and what to wear on a first date. She was very easy to talk to, was Kathleen, and always kept their secrets safe. It saved the embarrassment of talking to parents, particularly over more intimate matters. Kathleen took it all in her stride, happy to help whenever she could and assuming the role of agony aunt. She could have made a career of it if she hadn't been called by the culinary world. So many years sourcing ingredients while training as a chef on the Continent. She'd grafted primarily in France and Italy, honing her skills and creating meals, testing out different flavours based on the cuisine and traditions of the country she was in. An exciting and rewarding path to take, it was also challenging and sheer hard work.

Kathleen being Kathleen, there was always time for

Baker's Dozen

leisure and amusement and she led the field in extra-curricular activities, be it dancing, tennis or just socialising. Always popular wherever she went, she had no trouble in making friends, conversing with ease in another language.

In the closing stages of her career, she'd returned home to Britain and, after educating the masses in adventurous cooking, had finally settled in a West Country village, to play out the last of her days. Play, for Kathleen, was the operative word, as it had been all her life, despite the daily hours of toil. She had no intention of giving up, whatever her body repeatedly told her. Quite frankly its messages were becoming a nuisance, 'though at times they caught her unawares and momentarily dragged her down.

When young, she'd loved the odd lie-in (on the rare occasion her job afforded) after an exciting night on the town. Today the chance still seldom came as Kathleen frequently couldn't sleep, 'though why this should be, was a puzzle to her. This morning she was up early again. 6am. Same as usual. All old people are up early, she thought. Why is that? Do they need less sleep or are they now just restless after a life of worry, toil, experience and heartache? Good times too of course but it's the worries that keep you awake, that and wondering what comes next.

Did she turn the gas off before going to bed? Did she lock the doors? Did she check or did it even matter these days? Of course it mattered, Kathleen snorted to herself, jolting herself back to positivity, annoyed she'd thought

Baker's Dozen

otherwise. She had never been a negative person, all her life struggling to understand those who were and really having little time for them. She didn't suffer fools gladly, she chuckled.

Life was different now though. Harder somehow. Sometimes the mind, always the body. It was just as well that bus pass wasn't allowed until 9.30 as it took so long to get ready these days. All those years ago, skipping happily along the street as a little girl, she never thought she'd end up like this, creaking and wobbly. Goodness, it was an effort to get out of bed most days, especially when dark and the heating hadn't yet kicked in.

She always kept a dressing gown on top of the bed, that nice flannel one her friend had brought her back from her holiday in Scarborough. A strange present she'd thought at the time – people normally brought back shell animals or some local craft or other – but it had certainly seen some use this winter and she was glad of its warmth and comfort.

Using her bedside chair to steady herself, Kathleen stood for a moment, in her dressing gown and slippers, before moving off slowly towards the bathroom and then on downstairs, one step at a time, holding the rail on both sides while imagining herself downhill skiing, goggles on her head and slicing through the snow. *Bend zee knees*! If only she could!

Ooh, how she looked forward to her morning cup of tea. The first one of the day was always the best, a good

Baker's Dozen

Yorkshire brew, nice and strong. You wouldn't get that at the *après-ski*, that's for sure. More like a spritz or a bombardino. Kathleen had been skiing once and thoroughly enjoyed it, cutting a dash in her ice blue snow pants, attracting all the young men with her tall, sylph-like figure, carved turns and general derring-do. A long time ago now, for Kathleen had shrunk with the years and through recent ill health. Cancer had ravished her, thinned out her hair and left her a sorrowful shadow of her former upright self. Physically poor, her determination by contrast remained strong and she continued to dye her hair well into her eighties, bright colours to match her personality and outlook in life. Age and illness had diminished neither her spark nor her childhood wish to rule the world. Feisty still, she always won a debate and awoke each day ready to straighten out life's global problems. She could teach that government a thing or two, outwitting and outclassing them in knowledge, vision and skill and even showing them how to dress. Smart and chic was Kathleen with an Italian style derived from her years in Milan.

That was her task for today. A shopping expedition, to find a new outfit for young Saoirse's wedding. Something timeless that complimented her looks, her still warm smile and those blue eyes that sparkled. Spring chicken she was not, but what was wrong with an ageing hen in the winter of one's life? Yes, Kathleen decided, she could stride out with the best of them still. One foot forward and then the other, in three-inch heels and patent leather, Louboutin if she could get them. She'd paint her nails in her customary way, each one a different colour, her slender fingers adorned with rings that dazzled as they caught the light.

Kathleen smiled as she knew she'd outshine them, the wedding group in their modern clothes. Even the bride, in her off-white creation, was never a match for a daughter of Milan. Kathleen mused at the thought of her kitten heels as she glanced down at her furry slippers, cosy and warm on her bunioned feet. Feet that would take her upstairs again now, to prepare herself for the day ahead. Into the bathroom to wash all down, taking her time as she always did, easing the flannel over her body, nice hot water on dried-out skin. Then for the teeth, as the dentist ordered, upper and lower, back and front. It all took time and all took effort but couldn't be left and had to be done, however hard the task these days.

Bending over the sink was less of an option than it had been before but trying to stand upright for any length of time was not an easy task either. Kathleen worried that the day might come when she could no longer clean her teeth at all. Appearance had always mattered to her but she was still able to laugh at the sight in the mirror of a mouthful of potholes where teeth had once been. That was the character she was. Standing there now, with her Oral B, she weaved her brush in and out, like making lace on a dental doily. Gentle and slow to avoid more damage but ready now for

Baker's Dozen

a long sit down. The shopping spree would have to wait.

Not so the croissant that sat downstairs, beautiful just in its crescent form, its powdery surface calling her now. The light, soft centre irresistible, with lashings of salted butter on top. Don't tell the dentist she'd just cleaned her teeth, don't tell the doctor about the butter. Life was for living every step of the way and Kathleen was going to keep walking.

THELMA

Thelma Jackson was another of Andrew's favourites in the village and one he felt pleasure in chatting to. She'd lived there for some time, much longer than Kathleen, who'd only arrived in her latter years when seeking quiet and clean, fresh air to see her through her final days. Thelma, by contrast, had lived in the village for the last fifteen years of her working life and had carried on into retirement.

Thelma and Kathleen were very good friends, despite the dissimilar lives they'd led and a difference in age and temperament. They often met for afternoon tea, in the little café close to the church, with its tables covered in red gingham, its bone china cups and Viners cutlery. The service was always good there and the ladies felt they were well looked after as they chose from a menu of finger sandwiches, dainty cakes and fresh cream scones. They were sometimes joined by their female vicar, if her pastoral duties chanced to allow, or by one of the village retirees looking for scandal and local gossip. They wouldn't, however, find that here, as all three women were the soul of discretion and kept any secrets to themselves, however many they may have been told.

Baker's Dozen

Thelma had taught, all her life, and was used to hearing stories told. Some were true, others invented, be it teacher, pupil or parent narrating, personal tales or school related, several hundred over the years. She knew how to keep a confidence and knew when to seek advice or help without betraying the one who had trusted.

Thelma had worked up through the ranks, from her early days as a novice teacher, to Head of Department, to school headmistress. Her passion had been the subject she taught and she wanted her pupils to love it too. Art was Thelma's very world and she lived and breathed it every day of her life, hoping to instil her devotion in others. Some of her pupils had indeed been inspired, carrying it through to university, and had never lost touch with their favourite teacher, often visiting or sending cards and delighting her with their latest research. One had even been on TV, with a series about the Pre-Raphaelites and their medieval imagery.

Thelma loved all sorts of art and the way it could often provoke discussion. Art was a means of expressing oneself and it thrilled her to stand in front of a painting and look for clues to the story therein. Art could be such a powerful medium, giving voice to social or political views, and had often proved to be controversial in its new ways and experimentation. Many, she knew, didn't understand art and thought of its worth as purely subjective, but as long as they saw it as a feast for the senses, Thelma was happy to go with that.

Baker's Dozen

She'd travelled the globe in pursuit of her art, soaking it up through every pore, learning and loving each work she encountered of the famous collections around the world.

That very morning, when Andrew called with her crusty, home-made cottage loaf, Thelma was planning a trip up to town, to a new exhibition that she wanted to see. Any type of art enthralled her but surrealism fascinated, particularly the work of Salvador Dalí, none of whose art she had at home as it wouldn't sit well with the Rembrandts and Rubens. She loved his hallucinatory work and his use of double imagery and was looking forward to the exhibition immensely.

On arriving at the gallery, Thelma had headed straight for Dalí. She knew immediately she was in the right place as a giant poster of the man himself, sporting his famous upturned moustaches, loomed over her diminutive frame. She felt a little out of place in her smart two-piece and her hair in a bun and thought perhaps she should have dressed differently, to try and blend in with the showman's work. What indeed she might have worn was a subject she could always discuss with Kathleen, who was far savvier where dress was concerned.

So many paintings to admire and provoke, as Thelma ambled about the rooms, stopping reverently before each one, taking in each stroke of the brush and marvelling at the execution. She wasn't keen on the religious works, with the exception of *Christ of St John of the Cross*, its striking figure illuminated in an otherwise dark and curdled sky

Baker's Dozen

and depicted –unusually – from above.

She couldn't decide on her favourite piece as Dalí had just excelled at his craft, 'though she had a penchant for one or two and determined to buy a print from the shop. She settled on *Swans Reflecting Elephants* with its remarkable display of illusionism and its autumnal colours in a rocky landscape. Where she would hang this, she didn't quite know, but she knew that she simply had to have it.

After a well-earned cup of tea and a pastry that didn't disappoint, Thelma wended her way back home, ahead of the main commuter rush. She waited a while at her local station for a bus that never seemed to come before finally falling through the door, her Dalí print clutched in her hand. Her head was full of Salvador and she needed some time to sit and think.

She eased herself into her old comfy chair, moulded now to the contours of her body, and let out a small, happy sigh. What an interesting day it had been but she was certainly glad to be back home after so much walking and concentrating. She picked up her glass from the small, lacquered table and took a sip of the sweet-tasting sherry. Pedro Ximénez, one of Spain's finest, much like Señor Dalí himself.

Feet up on the stool, with its woven cover of Rembrandt's *Night Watch*, Thelma gazed around the room. She'd always liked this time of night, feeling contented, cosy and warm in the subdued lighting beneath the frames that showed off her Masters to utter perfection.

Baker's Dozen

She'd dispense that night with any cooking as nothing could match the food for the soul that she'd experienced in the gallery that day. Another sherry, then off to bed, to slip into one of Dalí's dreams.

The morning saw a perfect blue sky, the sun up before a rested Thelma, so soundly did she sleep that night after yesterday's more than pleasant adventures. She needed to walk and stretch her legs after so much shuffling and standing still. Just through the village was an ancient wood and that was where she decided to go.

The wood, for Thelma, was a form of beauty and very much alive in itself, with the echoing sound of a woodpecker knocking, and the occasional rustle amongst the leaves. Free to wander, she ambled along, breathing deeply and filling her lungs, with the sun slicing through the majestic trees and a gentle breeze upon the air. The whole scene was picture perfect and worthy of one of her frames at home.

She wasn't aware of how long she'd walked when something ahead of her caught her eye. She thought it was something she recognised 'though a somewhat deformed and unusual shape.

Thelma advanced with increasing caution as the scene unfolded before her eyes. A little clearing within the wood revealed a still and silent pool and, crouching at its very edge, a beautiful, young, naked male. As Thelma looked, he never moved but continued to gaze at the water before him. She stood and watched for quite some time, trying to

Baker's Dozen

decide what best to do, when all of a sudden he toppled in, the waters then closing swiftly above him.

In panic, Thelma reached the pool but not a trace of the man remained. There were no clothes on the woody floor, no marks where he'd sat and tumbled in. It was just as if he had never been.

Thelma knelt at the edge of the pool and plunged her arm beneath its waters, hoping to reach the body therein, but her wild thrashing was all in vain and Thelma knew that the youth was lost.

Arriving home in a frenzied state, Thelma slumped into her chair, disturbed and frightened by what she'd witnessed. The scene kept repeating within her head and she found that she couldn't block it out. Yet she felt she had seen the man before, gazing into that silent pool.

As she sat and looked around her room, for any comfort to ease her mind, Thelma spotted an open book. Looking up from the page before her, Dalí's *Metamorphosis of Narcissus*, depicting the ancient Greek myth of the man who had fallen in love with himself, in a reflection in a pool of water. Had the scene she had witnessed been true or was it her mind playing games?

Thelma went for a glass of water, shaking every step of the way. There in the kitchen, and new to her, stood a simple vase with a flower in – a single, bright, yellow narcissus.

MISS SCARLET

On Tuesday nights in the community hall, some of the villagers gathered together, for games, cards or just a drink, or generally a combination of all three. Annie and Jimmy were often there and Andrew always brought some cakes, freshly made from his bakery. He tried to vary the type he made and used his friends as guinea pigs when playing with new ingredients. Nothing outlandish, as he wasn't that kind of baker, but innovative all the same and they always went down well. The only one who refused to partake was a woman known to them all as Ruby – or Miss Scarlet to her venomous critics.

Miss Scarlet wasn't a Miss at all, having been married at least five times. "One more and she'll have the set, like Henry Eighth and his six wives", one of her neighbours unkindly said, 'though not expecting violent deaths. Ruby, like others, had many faults, but killing people to get her way could never be said to be one of them.

Something of the village diva, Ruby was full of her own importance, temperamental and hard to please. The archetypal femme fatale, she tended to eat her men for breakfast, luring them into her spider's web only to spit them out again. They came to her like moths to a flame, before she'd even uttered a word. Small and blonde with a bubble perm, a heart-shaped face and bright red lips, she tottered along in stiletto heels and outfits that belied her age. Nobody knew how old she was, 'though the village women had their opinions, given her past history. Some of course were mildly jealous, of her hourglass figure and breathy voice, but most just treated her as a joke, as one of the local characters. Their own Miss Scarlet from the Cluedo board, notorious for her many relationships.

At the present time, she was on her own, her latest divorce having just come through, but the scarlet woman was on the prowl, her eyelashes fluttering at every male. Technically a spinster now, unmarried and an older woman, Miss Scarlet ripped the rule book up as nothing could define her as an old maid, whatever the Oxford dictionary said.

Her eyes had fallen on Andrew once, at the time when he first arrived in the village, but she'd mistakenly come to see him as gay as he never seemed to be with a woman. She looked forward to his morning round, teasing him with her order for tarts, but Andrew could more than handle her, and not in the physical sense of the word.

Like many others, he found her fun, with a bubbly outlook that matched her hair, despite her occasional hissy fits. She had a certain *joie de vivre* and an attractive – to men – girlish giggle. He liked her for her *double entendres*, for the

Baker's Dozen

mischievous twinkle in her eye and never felt himself in danger from her over exuberant feminine ways.

The Cluedo board was out that night and four friends had gathered round to test their skills and guess who dunnit. Ruby sat in her usual chair, draping herself across the arm in a long, floaty, transparent creation that oozed with her beauty and sexual allure and showed off rather more than it ought.

Jimmy sat to the right of her, trying not to catch her eye or stare at the vision of gossamer. He'd had a close encounter before and, while he wasn't at all taken in, he'd loathe to have the scene repeated.

Annie and Andrew sat opposite them, their minds fixed on the Cluedo board, working out their different tactics and trying not to reveal their hand. They watched each time a sheet was marked, attempting to guess the rooms ticked off and waiting their turn to roll the dice.

Ruby was taking it seriously, checking for signs of any cheating and watching for any sleight of hand. She moved her suspect from room to room, trying to guess where the crime took place, by whom and with which weapon, before shouting her accusation out. She looked to see if her hunch was right, flouncing off in utter disgust when revealed to herself that her guess was wrong, eliminating her from the game.

Those in the hall not playing that night barely stirred at her show of anger, recognising the diva she was. Those

Baker's Dozen

at the table wanted her back as they needed her hand to continue the game. Jimmy went for a round of drinks while Andrew produced his almond cakes. Annie went to powder her nose while the others engaged in general chat.

They pondered whether to start a new game, as the drama queen failed to appear, but knew they'd only be part way through when she'd burst again upon the scene. They agreed it was better to keep the peace and wait for Miss Scarlet's triumphal return, however long she forced them to wait.

The three went and joined another group, leaving their game to gather dust in a now quiet corner of the room. The evening passed by in merriment, with no further talk of spanners and libraries, of whether the Reverend Green was innocent or a man of the cloth with a rotten core. Instead, they shared their holiday plans and looked to the summer months ahead.

At last the evening drew to a close and the games board was finally put away. The earlier game had gone unfinished and the real Miss Scarlet had not returned. Her non-reappearance was not unusual and nobody really thought much of it. Her storming out was typical if she wasn't seen to be getting her way. She'd played this role so many times that others took no notice now. The wind would blow and the sun would come out, just as it always had before.

Walking home at half-past ten, having taken his leave of Annie and Jimmy, Andrew saw a figure ahead. It dashed across the road in front, heading down towards the vicarage. What was he doing this time of night, if indeed it was a he, distance and the lack of light making it hard to ascertain.

Andrew carried on his way, towards the spot where the figure had run. Something in the air that night made him shiver and feel uneasy, as he reached the lane where the image had been. He stopped and looked from side to side, up and down the road before him, squinting his eyes for a better view. Nothing now presented itself and all was quiet in the lane. He stood there for a few moments more, listening out for any clues, but the silence of the night surrounded him, in an eerie way unencountered before. He shuddered and pulled his coat tight in, its warmth giving needed security.

Just as he turned to go on his way, a sudden movement up ahead, coming forth from the vicarage. Two figures now, running towards him, heading his way as he stood and stared. Very quickly they gained on him as Andrew was rooted to the spot, unable to move through sudden fear.

The vicar and her husband, out of breath, were bent over double in the lane before him. Waving her arms to attract attention, the vicar finally managed to speak: "Matthew's had an almighty shock" she was able to gasp while clutching her chest. "Ruby's dead and we've called the police."

Andrew appeared to have lost his voice as he opened

his mouth and let out a squeak. His eyes widened to twice their size as he tried to take in what the vicar had said. He could scarcely believe what his ears had heard, having only seen Ruby hours ago. The vicar shook him violently, trying to raise him from his stupor, having done the same only moments before when Matthew had stumbled through their door, mouth wide open and flailing his arms.

The vicar could always take control while all around her men were falling. She thought it must be part of her calling, always to know what to do, with practicality and presence of mind. Having now recovered her breath, the vicar set off, fleet of foot, the two men trailing along behind her.

When they reached the door of Ruby's house, the three stood still to compose themselves. Matthew described what had occurred, for the benefit of Andrew who was still in a daze. He'd been to dinner at Kathleen's house, his wife attending a meeting that night. Thelma Jackson was also there and the three had enjoyed a meal and a chat, poring over the day's events and between them putting the world to rights. Fish had been cooked, Dover Sole, and they'd washed it down with a crisp dry white. Kathleen was a fabulous cook, having trained as a chef in her younger days, as Andrew knew only too well, having been to dine with her many times.

Matthew had left around ten o'clock, pleasantly full from his evening meal and nicely relaxed from the cool white wine. He'd passed on by the community hall and the

Baker's Dozen

happy voices heard within, knowing his neighbours were having fun, enjoying each other's company.

As he'd walked on down the street, a light could be seen in Ruby's house. It flickered away in a downstairs room, a strange and somewhat ghostly glow that unnerved Matthew and made him think. Something didn't feel quite right and he'd decided to go and investigate. He'd never been a brave man, leaving adventure to his wife, but Matthew was a helpful soul and went and knocked at Ruby's door.

No reply to his several knocks had lured him round to the side of the house, to the room where the light continued to flicker. Peering cautiously through the window, Matthew had seen a candle alight, stood on a plate on the kitchen surface. Its flame threw shadows about the room as his eyes picked out familiar objects – a saucepan standing on the hob, a small table set for a meal.

Then it was that he'd spotted Ruby, sprawled across the kitchen floor, arms and legs at an awkward angle, her body's position quite unnatural. Matthew had reeled against the wall, his fist clasped firmly to his mouth, as he'd struggled to keep his emotions in and stop himself from being sick.

Moments later, he'd looked again and knew she must have breathed her last. A dagger skewered her very heart, its hilt once gleaming covered in blood.

Matthew had collected himself together and raced home

Baker's Dozen

to the vicarage. His wife was having a cup of tea, winding down after her meeting and working her way through a chocolate bar. This homely scene was suddenly shattered as Matthew told her the dreadful news.

The vicar had flown from her chair and phoned the police straightaway. Then she and Matthew had left the house, running to be ahead of them. That's when they'd met Andrew Baker, standing motionless in the lane.

A police siren wailed in the distance, as the three stood waiting anxiously. The vicar moved to the side of the house to see for herself the grisly scene but all she saw was an empty room, lights ablaze and no body.

As the police arrived, the front door opened and Ruby stood there facing them. Dressed in a bright red evening gown, she threw back her head and laughed at them. The night for her had ended well as she'd staged her own fake whodunnit. In a theatrical voice, she shouted out: "Miss Scarlet, the kitchen and the dagger!"

Ruby spent the night in a cell, her laughter echoing in everyone's ears, 'though none of them really saw the joke. A smart, young officer gave her a caution and suggested she might say sorry to her friends. As Ruby batted her eyelashes, she knew she was lucky to escape with a warning. She looked the officer up and down and wondered if he could be her sixth.

CERBERUS

Of all of those he knew in the village, there was one who truly stole Andrew's heart: Cerberus. Head and shoulders above the rest, the little Yorkie stood tall, a giant amongst dogs and humans alike for his loving, affectionate and playful nature.

Andrew had grinned when he'd heard his name, calling to mind the classical myth of the three-headed hound that guarded Hades, preventing the dead from ever leaving. It had taken the strength of Hercules to subdue the fierce and gigantic beast and carry him out of the Underworld. That Cerberus was named after him made Andrew smile when he saw the dog, his little legs trotting along, his head held high on full alert.

Cerberus' owner was known for his jokes and delighted in the name of his pet. If he'd owned a Great Dane, he'd have called him Tiny, for that was his waggish sense of humour. They were often seen in the village together, Cerberus and his devoted master, Bob in his chair, his pal alongside. Bob had been invalided out of the army, after a recent accident on active service, and had sought a friend to help him cope with his physical and mental injuries.

Baker's Dozen

Cerberus was a rescue dog, who didn't even have a name when found wandering the lonely streets. Looking for a human of his very own, he knew he'd found "the one" in Bob the moment he came to the animal shelter. Their eyes met in a crowded room and before long they were going home, the dog hitching a cheeky ride on his new dad's ready lap.

Andrew was glad to call at their house when carrying out his bakery round. It wasn't Bob who wanted bread, as it caused him bloating and abdominal pain. It was Cerberus who wanted his treats, which Andrew baked for him every day – a small handful of doggy biscuits, made in the shape of a tasty bone. Nothing toxic, nothing unhealthy, just simple, plain, basic cookies, small and crunchy as Cerberus liked. Andrew loved to hear the sound as Cerberus quickly devoured his treats, looking around for any spare.

A very protective little dog, he was often seen sat in the window, looking out at the passers-by and barking when anyone came to call. He took his job seriously, guarding the house like the dog-monster had, ever watchful and dutiful and deciding himself who to let in.

In appearance, however, they greatly differed, for the classical beast was a fearsome sight with his mane made up of a number of snakes, his serpent's tail and lion's claws. The little terrier was nothing like it, with his small frame and black and tan coat and a cold, wet, boopable nose. You wouldn't have touched the hell hound's nose, if indeed

Baker's Dozen

you could even find it amidst the writhing of all the snakes, but Cerberus was more amenable and loved to join in any game. He especially liked his tummy tickled and rolled over in readiness whenever a willing hand came near, which frequently it did.

It was for this cheery, fun and genial spirit that Bob sent him off once a week, to entertain and comfort the folk down at the home for the elderly. He took his turn on every lap, enjoying the strokes and fuss he was given and the odd treat here and there. He especially liked to be there for meals when a kind hand would slip him some meat or peanut butter on a spoon. His smooth tongue lapped it up and his eyes searched round for any more.

His eyes were some of his greatest assets. He knew it and he used them well. Soft, relaxed and full of expression, they showed his calm inner self and helped him secure whatever he wanted, be it food, a cuddle or just attention. The windows to his very soul, Cerberus' eyes were irresistible, appealing, big and deep with emotion. Born to be a therapy dog, he only had to look at you to make you feel happy, make you feel loved. His eyes did more than help him see, his eyes helped him to communicate and he accomplished that with great aplomb. So popular was the little Yorkie that the old folk looked forward to his every visit – more so than if their family had come (which often enough they didn't). It was hard to tell who enjoyed it the most: the elderly, for the companionship, or Cerberus for the snuggles and treats.

Baker's Dozen

He was good at seeing with his nose, that told him when there was food about or where another dog had been when it left its scent upon a tree. A form of mental stimulation, he liked his sniffs when out and about, smelling every post and wall and detecting scents both new and old. He sometimes left his calling card, to tell his friends that he'd been there, then checked the spot the following day to see if any had sent one back. Stop and start, stop and start, these stuttered walks were good for Bob, tagging along in his chair and halting at the favourite spots so Cerberus could have a sniff.

He liked to watch his little friend as he busied about on a patch of grass or ran back and forth enjoying himself. A happy dog was a happy Bob and he only wished he could get down with him instead of being confined to his chair.

Indoors, they had many games to provide them both with stimulus. Bob hid treats under cups or in different places around the house to see how quick the sniffer worked. He never could catch Cerberus out, as the little dog's powerful nose tracked the scent down every time. His keen nose work was second to none and kept him with a job to do, keeping him mentally and physically fit as he trotted round from room to room. He also liked a tug of war with a textured ring or bit of rope that he tried to wrestle from his dad, who always let him win the game.

Cerberus had many toys and was happy playing on his own as long as he knew that Bob was there. From snuffle

Baker's Dozen

mats to cute soft toys, from squeaky bones to chewy balls, Cerberus enjoyed them all. He sometimes chose to bury them, hiding them in a secret place, to return and enjoy them later on. Bob had had a dig pit made, that ran the length of his pretty garden and saved his plants from an unfortunate end.

He knew that Cerberus liked to dig and didn't want to discourage him as it kept him fit and motivated. He'd hide a few surprises there, to stop his friend from getting bored, and watched him as his paws went in, his head bent low in concentration. Cerberus was a natural terrier, digging away to his heart's content. Originally used as a ratting dog, in mines and mills throughout the land, the Yorkie could fit in a very tight space as it chased after vermin in slender burrows. Bob liked to watch Cerberus work, his front paws almost a blur as he dug and dug for all his worth, deeper and deeper in his garden pit.

His digging skills and sensitive nose had earned the dog a canine award when a child had gone missing from the village. A search had been mounted and the locals turned out, combing the lanes and nearby fields. For hours on end they'd looked for the boy and were on the verge of giving up for the day when Bob had suggested Cerberus.

They gave him the boy's shirt and jacket to help him determine his unique scent, then sent him off into the fields in the hope that he could track him down. Half an hour was all it took for Cerberus to find the spot. The boy had fallen through a cave and rocks had then crashed in on him, leaving him helpless at the bottom.

Cerberus' nose could smell him there and he dug and dug with all his might. So loud did he bark that it threatened to hurt his poor little throat, but louder and louder his voice became until the villagers caught him up. The child was rescued and taken to hospital where he was later to make a full recovery. Cerberus had saved the day and was recognised for his bravery in a special ceremony on the village green. He stood upon a podium, a new bandana on his chest and a box of treats awaiting him. "The bravest dog that ever there was" cried Bob as they all applauded him, taking his photo and shaking his paw while Cerberus took it all in his stride.

Bob himself was pleased as punch and glad to call the dog his own. Who would have thought, when they'd very first met, that Cerberus would save so many? He'd rescued Bob from loneliness, the old folk treated just the same and now he'd saved a little boy. The terrier with a heart of gold, a beautiful nature and a gift for love.

They spent a happy evening together, Cerberus playing in his pit and Bob in the garden admiring him. The child he'd saved often came by and took him for a country walk, when Bob was unable to manage it. Through the woods and fields they'd go, feeling the breeze as they journeyed along, enjoying the sun upon their backs. The boy could walk for miles and miles but Cerberus had little legs and sometimes

Baker's Dozen

had a carry back. How noble he looked in the child's arms, peering out at the world around him and planning his next great doggy adventure.

He'd need to get his strength up first and bedtime was starting to call. While Cerberus had his own comfy bed, which he used to nap in during the day, he preferred to join his master at night and always made sure he was in before him. A small pair of steps helped him up, as he couldn't jump the necessary height, and once there he chose his place, turning round upon the spot, deciding if it was suitable enough. After the spins, the digging started, the covers in perfect disarray, as Cerberus claimed his territory, making a safe and comfortable space. He settled down and went to sleep, dreaming of food and chasing squirrels. Bob lay down beside his friend, who was perfect in every possible way. A small dog with the biggest heart who came to him when needed most and had never not been there for him. A real companion, loyal and true, no wonder he was Bob's best friend. One man and his dog. What more in life could either of them need?

THE VILLAGE POST

The postman wasn't keen on dogs. He was more of a cat person himself, 'though he made an exception for Cerberus. He wasn't keen on bread either but he made an exception for Andrew, buying soft paninis and croissants for his beautiful wife at home.

He'd been the postie in the village for as long as anyone could remember and was held in great esteem by them all, for his punctuality, care with their parcels and ever courteous manner. He'd always go above and beyond and was a firm favourite with the elderly folk whose letters and cards he'd often take, to save them a walk to the post point. He'd even been known to put the stamps on, when the old ladies had forgotten to do so, paying out of his own pocket and never breathing a word. He loved them all and they in their turn loved him.

Ted was well into his fifties now, greying and weather beaten from years outside in every season. Come rain or shine, wind or snow, Ted could be seen walking the streets, postbag on his shoulder, striding out with a purposeful step. He was a fit man and a well man and changes in

Baker's Dozen

climate never bothered him.

When not on his round, he was in the garden or on his allotment, sowing potatoes and tending his beans, cutting the dahlias and mowing the grass. A practical man, like Andrew Baker, Ted could turn his hand to anything, having studied his father when growing up. When Andrew had first arrived in the village, Ted was the one who'd laboured for him, transforming himself from postie to brickie, digging foundations and mixing the mortar. The two had been friends ever since and were regularly seen on walks together, laughing and chatting as they went along.

They liked to swap stories of their delivery rounds but not in a gossipy way, more as a way of sharing experiences. Both were good at keeping a confidence and would never have revealed a secrecy. Their tales were often of days gone by and events that had happened outside of the village – funny occasions and strange occurrences, those with an air of mystery and those that were downright ordinary.

Ted, we know, wasn't keen on dogs and did his best to steer clear of them. He had good reason for this, having twice been bitten – once by an excitable, over-sized hound that tore through his stomach and had him hospitalised. He'd always been wary after that, even of small dogs if off the lead. Cerberus was a different beast, who knew Ted well and looked forward to him coming, taking the post in his gentle jaws and carrying it proudly back to his master.

Other visits were less endearing and one indeed was

Baker's Dozen

positively macabre. He'd called at a house with some letters one day, to have the front door opened by a lady dressed as the archetypal witch, in a long black robe and pointed hat. She took the post and beckoned him in, asking if he could come to her aid. He followed her, in trepidation, through a dark hall into the living room. The curtains were pulled and the light was dim. The walls were painted completely black and the air was musty as if something had died. As his eyes struggled and fought to adjust, revealed before him in the middle of the room was an open coffin with the body in. An actual corpse, stiffly laid and open to view, dressed in a formal mourning suit of dark cloth and charcoal striped trousers. Along its side ran a wooden cane with the remains of a tarnished silver top, once bearing the image of a wild and hornèd goat.

Ted had stared at the disturbing scene, unable to take his eyes away, till the woman beside him spoke again, her gloved hand pushing him forward.

What happened next, nobody knew, for when Ted came round, he was still in the room, lying dazed upon the floor, his head bleeding from an evident fall. Nothing around him looked the same. The curtains were open and light flooded in, the walls were painted a brilliant white and there was no sign of the woman or corpse. It took a while to steady himself and gently clamber to his feet. He slowly gazed about the room, till he spotted some paper upon the table – the letters that he had earlier brought. Someone there had opened them, the contents of one spilling out. A black-edged condolence card looked back at him with the chilling words: GONE BUT NOT FORGOTTEN.

The scene that he had witnessed that day stayed with Ted for the rest of his life. He discussed what had happened with several people, personal friends and professionals alike, but had never got to the bottom of it all and most likely never would. For Ted, the day had been shockingly real and nothing convinced him otherwise.

It was fortunate it happened only the once and he encountered no further weird goings-on. Most of his days were happily ordinary and nothing occurred to cause him alarm. There was plenty of scope for hilarity, mind, and he often told the tale to the ladies of a naked man opening the door, grabbing his post and running back in, hurrying to dress himself for work. Or of Annie and Jimmy as a panto horse, en route to their latest theatrical, the head galloping too fast for the body and coming apart at the side of the road. Such events made the postman's day and kept him chuckling as he went on his round.

Although he'd always loved his job, there were times when Ted had sometimes wished that someone would deliver his post to him. It seemed to take the excitement out when he brought his letters and parcels home, without the thrill of someone calling and greeting him with a bag of surprises. Some, of course, would not be welcome, the bills and flyers and piles of junk, but much of that would go in

Baker's Dozen

the bin, the same as if he'd brought it himself.

He thought of the post in former times and the fun of receiving a proper letter – handwritten with love and care. People rarely wrote these days, as digital means were now the rage. It was doubly special when a letter came, as it meant that someone had gone to the trouble of sitting down, with paper and pen, thinking through what they wanted to write, rather than bashing it out on a computer or a more recent handheld device. The author's pen was itself unique, each its own special manuscript, not like the fonts of the digital age that were much more uniform and less appealing.

The romance of receiving a handwritten letter, whatever its contents might disclose, was unrivalled in Ted's dreamy eye and led his mind down an ancient path of mail coaches pulled by magnificent horses, clattering over the miles at speed.

What sort of men were the coachmen of old, the drivers and guards that raced through the night, blowing their horns on arrival and departure, at stages and inns along the route. Ted would have liked to experience that, to ride out on top, on the driver's box, in heavy rain and howling winds, urging the four strong horses on. Different by far from his warm, cosy van with its bright red coat and alloy wheels!

So many changes over the years and doubtless many more to come. He'd often mused on the ways of the

Baker's Dozen

world and the manner in which people saw themselves. Everyone wanted a fancy name, a title to make themselves sound important, to add an air of gravitas to an otherwise ordinary and mundane job. It didn't alter the tasks therein, their duties and responsibilities, but kept some happy and made others laugh as they tried to guess what the titles meant, like passenger service agent or care negotiator, or community outreach and engagement officer. A fine mouthful of words that wouldn't fit on an envelope when corresponding through the post and doubtless didn't increase their pay.

What could he, as a postie, become? A despatch, parcel and packet porter? A mobile missive and epistle bearer? Or simply a correspondence carter? The list was seemingly endless.

It was almost a way of donning a disguise, of becoming someone else for the day, while the routine job carried on, much the same as it always had. With this in mind, he approached young Jimmy to see if anything could be done.

Jimmy and Annie, the re-enactors, who loved nothing more than dressing up, were only too ready to come and assist and help him to realise his cherished dream. Nobody – save Andrew – in the village was told, as the four prepared to put on a show.

It took the friends some time to arrange, being far from a run of the mill event and needing input from several sources. First, they went to a local museum to see if a coach

Baker's Dozen

could be hired out, and then to one much further afield where an ex-Army man was willing to help. He also knew of a team of horses that were regularly used for public displays and were capable of pulling a heavy load. Four fine Percherons, a large, muscular, draft breed of horse, were offered up to pull the coach and the posse of friends jumped at the chance.

Their next move was to visit a costumier, who Annie and Jimmy already knew, through their various trips with the re-enactment society. Suitable dress was quickly found and all four friends were kitted out, Andrew being the more timid of the party, not really partial to dressing up. For Ted, however, he would make an exception, as Ted was one of Andrew's best friends.

The weeks went by and the day came round for Ted's dream to be realised. The villagers suspected nothing, so closely had the secret been guarded. The rattle of wheels woke them up as the mail coach rumbled down the street, joined by the clatter of horses' hooves and the powerful blast of an old post horn.

Up on the box seat, next to the driver, sat Ted the postman in splendid array. His black hat with a gold band complemented his scarlet coat with its blue lapels and intricate braid. Andrew rode shotgun, on full alert, scanning the street for any attack while Annie waved from inside the coach, in her long gown, bonnet and shawl.

How sumptuous it all looked – the coach in its polished

Baker's Dozen

livery, the upper part black and its wheels in red, its lower panels and door in maroon, displaying the royal coat of arms. Pulled by the four grey Percherons with well-muscled legs and a deep, wide chest, the coach came through at eight miles an hour, those aboard being jostled and jarred as it made its way round the village streets.

A horseman suddenly rode into view, his face masked and travelling at speed. Jimmy, dressed as a highwayman, galloping fast as if fit to burst and waving a make-believe flintlock pistol. The coach halted before his horse and Ted jumped down to deliver the post, as Annie was swiftly carried up and left on the back of a spirited steed.

The coach then continued on its way, Ted now blowing his old post horn, its brass gleaming in the early morning sun, mirroring the gold on his hat and coat. A smile was spread across his face as the villagers all came out to look – at Ted in his much-loved uniform, riding atop a beautiful coach. Before too long, he was out of sight, the horses bearing the postman away, his dream now become a reality.

THE OUTSIDER

Faisal was a poet. He was foreign and bohemian and stood out in the village, not just for this but for the way that he dressed, in his baggy harem pants and his long flowing shirts, his refusal ever to wear a tie and his hair held back in a ponytail. He looked like no one they'd ever seen, not in the local vicinity anyway, and some weren't sure if they wanted him there. He didn't look like the villagers, he didn't even sound like them with his Near-Eastern accent and nervous English. He was, they said, a cog in a wheel that didn't fit and capable of upsetting the applecart. The village may not have been ready for Faisal but he was ready for them.

The son of agèd immigrants, Faisal had come with them to Britain, prepared to start a new life in the West and to leave his troubled country behind. They'd settled at first in a Midlands town where his parents had worked in the textile industry, creating batiks and dyeing cloths, toiling away to earn their crust, every hour that Allah sent.

Faisal, by contrast, had drifted along, not really knowing where he slotted in, with no job and no money, preferring

Baker's Dozen

instead to sit in a field, looking up at the clouds and dreaming. Hours could pass without him knowing, as he sat in the grass with the flowers and bees, humming along with their summer tune. He watched as the birds swooped and dived, hearing their call and learning their song, as they wheeled to and fro in the evening sky.

It was here that he'd first started to write, initially only in his head, committing to memory the lines he composed, before setting forth with paper and pen. Short pieces, to capture his mood and the natural world that enfolded him:

> *"Alone on a bank*
> *But not alone, for the bees*
> *Keep me company."*

Nature and wildlife spoke to his soul, wrapping their very arms around him, smoothing away any aching sorrows and caressing him with their gentle touch. There was nowhere else he wanted to be, as the butterflies circled about his head, pausing awhile to share their beauty with this calm, quiet and tender man. His naked feet upon the grass, connecting with the earth itself, enjoyed the feel of the air that lapped softly and lightly over his skin. His inner being was filled with peace as he watched some ants at their evening toil:

> *"Barefoot in the grass*
> *A busy ant hurries by*
> *Tickling my ten toes."*

Baker's Dozen

It was only later, when his parents died, that Faisal knew he must move home, far away from his Midlands town and closer to nature in a small village. He liked the look of Little Bunting from the very first moment he saw it online and felt that he could be happy there. A small plot of land was quickly purchased, with the inheritance from his mum and dad, at the edge of the village, near Andrew's house. He next bought himself a campervan, which was where he now intended to live, simply and frugally in the countryside around.

Andrew had called, on his first day there, with a pint of milk and some homemade bread. The two had immediately formed a bond, through their love of nature and wildlife, and would often talk into the night, as they listened to the sound of a distant owl calling its mate from a faraway tree. Faisal made Andrew a friendship bracelet, which he always took great pains to wear, to thank him for such a thoughtful act and to show just how much it had meant to him.

Thelma was attracted to Faisal too, for his love of art and passion for music. She'd often heard him, alone in the evening, sitting inside his camper van, gently tapping a tambourine, the jingle of its metal zills softly quaking in the cool night air. At other times, a plaintive lament, one of his own compositions, played with feeling on the concertina, as his hands moved slowly in and out. Thelma loved to hear him play and could have stood in the field all night, the melancholy airs drifting over her, lulling her into a sense of peace.

Baker's Dozen

Not all of the villagers felt that way and some had become rather hostile. They didn't like his campervan, his laid-back ways and his means of living, his wandering round in a dream-like state and his unconventionality. Never mind that he paid his way, that he'd bought the land that his van was on, that this man from the East was a gentle soul with positive values and a heart of gold.

Ken the builder and his wife Darlene were loud in their dislike of him, encouraging others to be the same and rejoicing at their apparent success. Kenny liked a man's man and Faisal didn't fit the bill, with his long hair and effeminate ways and absurd liking for poetry. He wore a necklace, for heaven's sake, a silver chain with a Celtic cross, a shirt with beads and mirrors sewn on, and tie-dyed pants that he'd made himself. What sort of a man went out like that? None that Ken and Darlene knew.

They tried to get the vicar on board but she was having none of it and told them to go and think again and not coerce anyone else. So they turned instead to Major Morton, who liked his rules and conformity, everything in order and in its place. Faisal he deemed to be out of order and out of place in a quiet country village like this. He set to, with a rallying cry, to make the poor man feel unwelcome, cutting him out of every event like taking scissors to a paper form. No invitations came Faisal's way to any community-based occasion, to socials in the village hall or dinner parties and barbecues.

Baker's Dozen

Until, it was, the vicar saw red, and Andrew came to hear of it too. A special dinner was organised, with Faisal as the guest of honour. They held it at the vicarage with a number of friends and neighbours there. Each guest did a party piece, which ranged from the ordinary to the frankly bizarre, to lighten the tone and spread some humour and to make Faisal feel at home and at ease.

The vicar gyrated to some funky music while Matthew balanced a spoon on his nose. Andrew juggled with eight bread rolls before dropping the lot in Thelma's lap, and Kathleen performed a conjuring trick. When dinner was finished, they formed a line and congaed out and into the street, the vicar leading with Faisal behind, his flip flops flapping as he moved his feet.

Kathleen watched as they went up and down, her dancing days behind her now, but cheered as loud as her voice would allow, as her friends congaed on into the night, every so often taking a pause for Thelma Jackson to catch her breath. Thank goodness she'd worn her sensible shoes, for her feet would be in a sorry state. It was Faisal's turn to take the lead, and striking with force his tambourine, he led them on in a constant rhythm, marking the beat as they progressed on.

The scene was witnessed from several windows and, one by one, doors were flung open, as villagers poured out into the street, extending the snake as they joined its tail, zigzagging down to Andrew's house and back again to the vicarage.

Baker's Dozen

Major Morton looked on aghast, with Ken and Darlene at his side. What had happened to their quiet village and why was the vicar involved in this? Her husband, Matthew, should take her in hand before she was lost and out of control. This was surely Faisal's fault, with his lax and corrupt foreign ways.

If truth be known, the Major had never really been keen on the vicar, from the moment she first arrived in the village. Women should know their place, he thought, and were better off cleaning the pews and arranging flowers, not standing and preaching from the holy altar. As time had gone on, he had come to accept her, not least because she was good at her job – very good in fact – but Faisal was a step too far. His poems were even appearing in the church newsletter, although he hadn't seen him ever set foot in there!:

"Beauty and quiet
Meditation, thoughts and prayers
In this house of peace."

It didn't even rhyme!

The Major and Kenny were crusty old sorts, stuck in their ways and always complaining. Nothing was ever right for them and their only pleasure was to have a good moan. The vicar dancing in the street, with Faisal's hands about her waist, was really beyond the pale. Yet Matthew didn't seem upset, joining in at the back of the line! This was all very

Baker's Dozen

unseemly and far too liberal in the Major's mind.

The following day, he spotted Faisal at the door of his van, chatting to Andrew. The latter had just been delivering bread and Faisal was handing something back. Not the customary coins or notes but a small, brown, paper bag. Andrew seemed to be pleased with it, as he held it aloft in a thumbs-up way, nodding and smiling as he carried on his round. Later in the morning, Faisal was seen, with a similar bag at Thelma's house.

This, to the Major, was interesting, and he made it his mission to investigate. Over a coffee, he enlisted Darlene, to pay a surprise call on Thelma. The women had never been close friends since Darlene had laughed at a Salvador Dalí that Thelma had bought at an exhibition. "Swans look nothing like elephants!" Darlene had jibed as she stared at the print in utter incredulity. Thelma had tried, in vain, to protest, but Darlene had closed her ears to her now and had launched a tirade on Spanish art.

Thelma was surprised to open the door to a woman she'd barely seen since then. Darlene stood, in an all-white jumpsuit, rattling a fake collection tin. Her feet in the hall, without being asked, Darlene headed straight for the kitchen, where Thelma had started making her lunch. The smell of bacon pervaded the air and something else cooked in the frying pan. "I can't stop long" Darlene said, as Thelma set out her knife and fork.

"I'm having the mushrooms that Faisal brought"

Baker's Dozen

Thelma replied, happily. "He collects them, you know, he's a forager, and often brings those that he's found to me."

Darlene knocked the pan from the hob and the mushrooms scattered across the floor. Her eyes open wide and horrified, she ran from the house at breakneck speed, convinced that Thelma was being poisoned. That meant Andrew was poisoned too, as Faisal had also delivered to him.

Thelma was left without her lunch as she picked up the food from the kitchen floor. She then rang Andrew to tell him the news that Darlene was undoubtedly heading his way. Andrew sighed as the doorbell rang but left his guest to open the door. Faisal and Darlene, face to face, was a sight that many had wished they'd seen. One out of breath and splattered in oil, the other holding a chanterelle.

Andrew pulled them both back in and set Darlene down in an easy chair. Faisal brought her a cup of tea, which after a lot of coaxing from Andrew, she readily drank from her shaking hands. They talked about caps, stems and gills, of spores and rings and funnel shapes, of knowing where to look and when and which to pick for a tasty meal. Over time, Darlene came round, 'though much of the talk went over her head. Faisal offered a mushroom feast with ceps, morels and parasols and promised not to poison them all.

The meal was held in an open field, with the neighbours sat on woven rugs that had come from Faisal's parents' house. In warm-coloured clothes to match his heart,

Baker's Dozen

Faisal won them round that day, in his gentle, caring and compassionate way and his capacity always to forgive. In a quiet voice, he read to them, to thank them for finally letting him in:

> *"A tender embrace*
> *To you each is extended.*
> *Love surrounds us all."*

MR AND MRS PRIMA DONNA

It was Tuesday and Kenny was having a moan. It could just as easily have been a Thursday or a Friday, it mattered not, for Kenny had a moan every day of the week. More than one, sometimes. His wife, Darlene, would join him in this for the pair were two of a kind.

They'd met years ago, on a stag weekend, in a sunny, coastal resort in Spain. Kenny was there as part of a group. One of his crowd was getting hitched and they were boozing their way through his last days of freedom. They weren't into the Spanish wines, real *sangría* or delectable sherries; instead they were downing cheap, foreign beer that tasted of nothing and gave you a headache. The only food they consumed that night was fish and chips from an olde English pub and an unauthentic Spanish *paella* with no fish and no meat, undercooked rice and hard, frozen peas.

In the same resort, Darlene from the States, there with some friends for a bachelorette and a whistle-stop tour of Western Europe. Shimmering in sequins and painfully high shoes, the women tottered about the town, dressed to kill and ready to party. Only one was about to wed, 'though

Baker's Dozen

the others were all very much on the lookout – for an olive-skinned, Spanish male, dark haired and dark eyed, with pots of money if he could possibly manage it.

Both parties had lain all day in the far too hot summer sun, dashing in and out of the sea, then back under the beach parasols, as red as their bodies had now become but less aglow in the evening light.

Easing themselves into the bar that night, the women had spotted the men at once – raucous, rowdy and flashing the cash as they shouted for ever more beer and chips. The poor Spanish waiters ran to and fro, wishing they worked at another bar, but glad that they had a job at all, so high was the unemployment rate. They winced at the ill-cooked food served up and the litres of drink that were being consumed, and longed for the hours to drain away, to pull down the shutters and leave for home, for a restful night and a hopeful new day.

The women's group was becoming loud and shrieks of laughter filled the air as one or two tried out their Spanish on the ever-patient but weary waiters. Then clutching their drinks in sunburnt hands, they made their way to the table of men who shunted about to allow them in. Not a single olive-skinned male amongst them, no lithe and brave toreador, dressed to impress in his suit of lights lying tight on his slender body. Instead, a pack of beer-bellied men in knee-length shorts and gaudy shirts that clashed with their red, peeling skin from a day spent grilling on the sand.

Baker's Dozen

Something, there was, in the air that night, or perhaps they were slipped a Mickey Finn, as none of them noticed each other's burns as they partied into the early hours, sinking their drinks and eating their chips. The stars must also have been aligned, as Kenny found his wife-to-be, claiming the stag do for his own and leaving the original buck in the lurch.

Ken and Darlene were a pair well-matched, shameless and brash, audacious and brazen. Darlene had been an actress once but had failed to win any leading parts and had fallen foul of a dozen directors for her erratic behaviour and manipulative ways.

The two had married within a month in a quick ceremony with no guests. None were invited, so none came, and the pair tied the knot surreptitiously. It had startled them all in Little Bunting when Kenny had first brought his new wife home. Some were surprised he had married at all as they thought there was none who would take him on, while others were amazed that he'd hooked such glamour – a former Hollywood actress, no less. What on earth did she see in him, with his ugly physique and crude, course ways, his crumpled face and strident voice?

Tinseltown may have chucked her out but Little Bunting did its best to welcome this artist to its bosom. For a time, they truly feted her, making her seem the star of the show, cutting ribbons at local events, presenting awards at the country fair. Kenny paraded her round the streets,

Baker's Dozen

reminding them who this woman was and showing her off as a cut above. He started to assume great airs himself, belittling those he had called his friends and adopting a somewhat superior stance.

His first target was Andrew Baker. It was Tuesday and Kenny was having a moan. The breakfast sourdough he'd ordered for Darlene had not been delivered at the time it should and his wife was having a temper tantrum. His calls to Andrew had gone unanswered and the little patience he'd had, had snapped. His nostrils flared and his face turned red as he crashed about in their terraced house, cursing the man for his shoddy service. Darlene was becoming hysterical now, forced to endure a day-old loaf that she saw as only fit for the bin. The baker, she thought, should lose his job, for this wouldn't have happened back home in the States.

When Andrew called, ten minutes late, he found the remains of a loaf on the path. Yesterday's bread, thrown with force, had landed beyond their garden gate and was now being pecked at by hungry birds. The door flew open and Kenny flew out, shouting abuse as Andrew approached. His wife was behind him, egging him on, in a bizarre display of arrogance. Neither listened to Andrew's words as he tried in vain to explain the delay, keeping his calm in a sea of fury as the insults from the pair kept coming. In desperation, he walked away, leaving the bread on a small side wall, causing a further stream of expletives.

Baker's Dozen

Darlene knew how to put on a show and many, at first, had been taken in, dazzled by her glamour and glitz, her flamboyant ways and ostentation. She appeared to be kind when it suited her, to worm her way into someone's affections, but she just as easily spat them out when she'd had her fill and was moving on. Such was the case with Mary Sue, who'd befriended her when she first arrived, joining her for cocktails after work and trips to the local cinema. The two had seemed to hit it off, till Darlene learnt who her parents were and had shunned and ignored her ever since. The Freebies never paid their way and Darlene, like others, was annoyed at that.

One by one, she pushed friends away – gradually, so that no one noticed. It was like she was at a seaside arcade, shoving the coins over the edge, rejoicing as each was detached from the rest.

But soon her glitter started to fade as the villagers got the measure of her. First to realise was Thelma Jackson, always quick to work it out from her years spent as a school headmistress. Nothing and no one would get past Thelma, with her clear judgement and intellect. Open to welcoming somebody new, especially one from another culture, she'd greeted Darlene with her usual warmth, including her in any social event.

Often, the two took tea together, at the village café or at Thelma's house. Darlene had joined her for art exhibitions, claiming a knowledge of the Baroque movement. Her

Baker's Dozen

mask, however, was quick to slip, and she was unable to join in the conversation, when Thelma discussed her love of Rembrandt and his style akin to Caravaggio. Darlene was all window dressing as she stuttered and stumbled, lost for words, as Thelma continued her monologue. The die for Thelma was finally cast when Darlene mocked her Dalí print, failing to grasp its illusionism and treating his artwork as a joke.

Darlene was such a prima donna, her husband the male equivalent, never recognising the trait in themselves but very quick to see it in others. Self-absorbed and self-important, ignorant, demanding and asinine were some of the labels applied to them as the villagers of Little Bunting woke up.

They witnessed the clash of the petulant divas as Darlene met Ruby face to face, rebuking her for the fake whodunnit that made the neighbourhood think she was dead. That in itself had ignited the fire as Ruby, in turn, rounded on her, pouring scorn on her acting skills as an unfulfilled Hollywood superstar.

Ruby was bubbly and very creative, harmless and fun in a childlike way, tolerated throughout the village as a colourful, spirited and outlandish vixen. Darlene, however, went more to extremes, sharp-tongued and cruel and full of herself. Simple, but not in an infantile way, she was seen as intellectually deficient, easily fooled and slow to catch on.

This, to Kenny, was unimportant, cast from the same

Baker's Dozen

mental mould, none too bright and pretty gormless but doting on his actress wife. Content to follow in her wake, he looked like a helpless and loyal pup, anxious to please and waiting on treats.

The pair had teamed up with the army Major, the only military man in the village and, like themselves, insatiable. Ever ready to lead the charge, he was an active and obstinate troublemaker who'd lick the lot of them into shape and iron out their lackadaisical ways. Someone had to take command and he was just the man to do it.

Change had blown through the neighbourhood, of a most unfitting and unorthodox kind. First the vicar and then the poet, in an otherwise unremarkable shire. The Major was known to jump to conclusions before giving anyone the benefit of the doubt – feet first, head after (if the head was to follow on at all). He'd wrongly judged the vicar's abilities and wrongly judged the foreign bard, and was forced to admit he'd made a mistake, not just once but twice in a row.

Aiding and abetting on this wrong-footed path, the know-it-all diva Darlene, who'd wrongly accused a man of poison before eating and enjoying the evidence. Where was her faithful dog in all this? Curled at her feet, awaiting his treats! Faisal had claimed a victory that day with his fungi and his smooth poet's tongue – a good enough reason for Darlene to moan and wait for her husband Ken to join in. It was a Tuesday after all!

BROWN BREAD

The door was almost closed now. Lying there, anguished and still, in her bed, Gabriella was deep in thought. The door had been closing for some time and she had watched it happening, powerless to do anything about it. She had tried. Many times. Of course she had. Of course she had tried, but to what end? It had made no difference. Except to her. It had made her worse, by labouring.

What did it matter to anyone else? There was no one else for it to matter to. Gabriella was on her own, as she had been now for some time. Trying and struggling. Trying and struggling and making herself hurt. But what could she do? She had to try, had to give it a go, 'though she knew it would make no difference. She'd known that really for quite some time but had almost blinded herself to it, in her efforts to return to normal.

But what was normal? She felt she no longer knew. Perhaps she never had. Perhaps she had been mistaken. All these years, so many of them now, in what she had thought was normality, in what she had thought was happiness, only to find she was wrong, that she'd somehow been

Baker's Dozen

deceived and made to look a fool.

Had other people seen it? Seen the way this was going? Why did nobody tell her? Or why had she closed her ears? Yes, perhaps that was it, she hadn't wanted to hear, hadn't wanted to know. Life was full of change. She'd accepted that before. Often embraced it, even. But this was change with a difference. Change she didn't want. Change being forced upon her, clamping her in its jaws.

Her head was full of thoughts, kept her awake at night, troubled her during the day. She couldn't block them out. They'd taken her over now. Held her like a prisoner, bound her up in chains, fastened her to a lock and thrown away the key.

But had she ever held the key? Had she ever known the truth? Did she know it now or did she still decline to believe? She had never felt alone but she certainly felt it now. Alone with her innermost thoughts. Why had they left her here? What had she done wrong? Had she done any wrong, committed some heinous crime? She knew in her heart that she hadn't but could hear the voice within. Over and over again, the thoughts went round in her head. They twisted, turned and knotted and she couldn't sort them out.

The drumbeat began again as she repeated her daily mantra:

"*I am not a bad person. I am not a bad person. I am not a bad person.*"

Baker's Dozen

Who was she saying it to? Who did she want to convince? She'd written it up on her fridge but that was long ago now. If only the door would open, if only by a crack. But it wasn't going to happen.

Gabriella had always been kind, kind to everyone. Some were kind to her and she cried every time that they were, cried for the joy of it all, tears streaming down her face. But now she wasn't wanted and she couldn't work out why.

Why, why, why, why, why? Why was "why" such a difficult word? Why, oh why, oh why. It didn't even sound like a word, the more you heard it said. Why. Why?

She'd been cut out of life forever, as if someone had taken the scissors, followed the dotted lines in the shape of a little figure. But what to do with the cutout? And what of its remains?

She lapsed in and out of sleep but never for any time. Those thoughts just kept her awake, busied themselves in her head, like bees round a honeypot but nothing like as sweet. If there were only a way to find out where it had all gone wrong. But that was a hopeless cause as Gabriella knew only too well.

She found herself on the rack, tortured with so much pain, as a hand kept turning the wheel and tightened its ugly grip. Too much agony now, in her body and in her brain, in her heart and in her soul, in the very fibre of her being.

She'd seen the pattern forming, as in the Arans she used to make. Knew where it was going, could see the end ahead.

Baker's Dozen

Her knitting had not been easy but this was something again. Not a pleasant stitch within it, not a cosy, nice, warm feel and only her to see it, no one to share the end.

She'd watched her life unravel, as she'd tried her best to see, but her eyes refused to open, however hard she tried. Perhaps, after all, there was nothing there to see, and it was all in her troubled mind. A hallucination, a trick of the light, a haze on a far horizon.

She should have taken the bus, the moment she fell ill. The bus to Switzerland, the bus to the other side. Perhaps she'd have slept on the journey, more than she slept at home, or perhaps she'd have sat awake, thoughts running through her mind. There'd be time enough for sleep – the big sleep later on – but would she ever awake, ever see again?

Who else would be on the bus? A companion for her journey? Or would she sit alone, just as she lay here now? Would she find some comfort in the bleakest darkness there was? Would there be a light, to guide her on her way?

"Though I walk through the valley of the shadow of death..."

Her mind tossed and turned in her delirious state, disturbed by the thoughts going round in her head. The wind outside rattled the glass and the door closed further still. It wasn't the wind that had pushed it to, but a hand that she knew, that was out of sight.

Her mental condition was teasing her, as she thought of the person behind that hand. The one who was trying to

Baker's Dozen

shut her out, to cast her adrift in a bottomless boat, to hope that she sank beneath the waves, never to rise up again.

Gabriella struggled to free herself from the torments that tangled her brain. She hurt both physically and mentally. The latter she could do without, the former she could manage. Both were constant and both were great but one outstripped the other by far.

Back and forth, on a restless wave, her mind was tripping her up again. She couldn't keep herself afloat, gasping for air in her frenzied state. How had it ever come to this and when would she ever be released?

She wished that God would take her now, to end her present misery, and tried to raise her hand to the sky in the hope that He would bring her in.

There were no winners and losers here, however she cared to look at it, but the weight of sadness dragged her on, further into the slough of despond. Gabriella's thoughts overwhelmed her now, as she lay quite stiff in her single bed. Her demons refused to leave her alone, unlike everyone else she knew. Random thoughts popped into her head and out again the other side, splattering themselves upon the walls and ending up in a further mess.

Discomfort with herself remained as she looked back over the last few months. When did the canker start to grow and when was she first affected? The affliction, she knew, wasn't physical, but derived from an entirely different source and from one she could not escape. There it was,

Baker's Dozen

until the last, laid over her like a heavy blanket, starting to suffocate.

She'd done her best, she really had, but it was far too late for that now. The door was taking its final steps and would soon be shut for good. There was nothing left to prop it open, nothing to halt its stride. It relentlessly carried on its way, staring her in the face.

Her eyes looked around for one last time, as she pulled the sheet up close. Her agonies never faded away, her spirit in constant turmoil. What could she do to make amends, if amends were needed to be made? What could she do to gain some peace and quell her violent storms?

Gabriella's energy was leaving her now, sapped at its very base. There was little time to think or cry, just be ready to give herself up. Gabriella knew she had flaws enough and prayed they had been accepted. For who amongst us is ever perfect, who is wholly good? Love, she knew, was encompassing and love would win in the end.

The following day was a commonplace one, nothing to set it apart. The world carried on as it always had and, no doubt, as it always would. The sun came up to greet the dawn but quickly disappeared, to be followed by rain and brooding skies as life just rumbled on. The postman out on his daily round, the vicar at morning prayer, Cerberus cocking his leg by a wall while Bob sat in his chair. Nothing amiss or untoward, nothing to raise alarm, nothing to cause the bells to ring or prompt a crowd to form.

Baker's Dozen

Down through the village, Andrew came, swinging his bag of bread. He hummed to himself a happy tune, unsurprisingly unsuspecting. Several times he knocked at her door, before thinking that something was wrong. The curtains were drawn and the lights were off and the house held a deathly silence. In the distance, a haunting lament on Faisal's flute drifted across a lonely field in the early morning air.

Andrew stood at Gabriella's front door and slowly bowed his head, the brown loaf in his hands no longer warm but already cold to the touch. He knew she had passed away.

Andrew later laid flowers at her door – but they died in the summer heat.

THE CLOCKS

(A DAY IN THE LIFE OF LOTTIE)

5 am. Starting as a gentle purr, it quickly graduated to a loud, intermittent meow before rising to a clamorous and prolonged wail. Chester the cat was bored and threatening to wake the dead. He'd been on his own all night and now he'd had enough. He wanted someone to play with and he knew just where to find them. Up the stairs he went, along the top passage, pushed the door open and jumped upon her bed. He meant to wake her up and wake her up he did

Chester was the first of her clocks to go off and the signal for the day ahead. A silver-grey, large Chartreux, he'd lived in the house for a couple of years and was very much at home. Lottie's sister had brought him from France when his owner could no longer care for him. Now aged four, he ruled the roost and, although his breed was usually quiet, he proved the exception to the rule – early in the morning at least.

A playful biff upon the nose had Lottie throwing the covers back. Time to get up and start her day and see what

Baker's Dozen

would unfold. First on the list, Chester the cat, wanting to go outside. Bare footed, she went downstairs, opening the door to his garden. Bleary-eyed, she crossed to the fridge, taking out the milk for her tea and Chester's fresh chicken. He wasn't, *he* thought, a fussy eater, just knew what he liked and knew what he didn't, and chicken topped his list. Where was the harm in that?

Ablutions over, he ambled in and headed for his bowl, waiting with an expectant look as Lottie chopped up his meat. A few mouthfuls and a sip of water and Chester was off again.

Lottie, meanwhile, put on the kettle to make a cup of tea. Shuffling about, scarcely awake, she knew she had only minutes now, before the alarm from her radio clock went off, at 5.30 on the button, prompting the next job on her list. Her elderly dog, in his comfy basket, stirred at the sound of the newscaster's voice, but barely raised his head. Twelve years old in doggy years, nudging seventy in human, he didn't venture far these days, preferring to lie in a nice, warm kitchen, dreaming of carefree puppy days. How cosy he looked, with his head resting on his paws and his Basset Hound ears concertinaed around them. It seemed such a pity to disturb him there but Lottie knew he must get his exercise, however short and however slowly. Gently stroking him on the head, she left him for now to drift back to sleep while she poured her tea and attended to the washing.

How did the pile become so big? There were only four

Baker's Dozen

of them in this house but their clothes formed a veritable mountain. She and her mum didn't change that much, but the girls churned out clothes like a sweatshop. Sportswear, casual wear, uniforms and posh frocks, trousers, blouses, skirts and nightwear. Where did it all come from and why did they only wear it once? Lottie never bothered to sort it out. The whites went in with everything else and had to take their chances these days. Round and round in the drum it went, like her list for today in her dizzying head.

The ironing pile awaited her next, just as big and just as daunting. Inevitably, most would be left again, as she concentrated on today and the clothes that were needed for school. She wouldn't have her girls look crumpled, however creased she looked herself, and sent them forth into the world nicely ironed, smooth and neat. They rarely stayed that way of course, but at least they were not alone in that, their schoolmates looking just as ruffled, when the bell rang to end their day.

7 am. Right on time, regular as clockwork, Andrew Baker knocked on the door, carrying a large, white, sliced loaf. Hooray for his punctuality, his nice warm smile and nice warm bread. Sadly never time to chat, as lunches needed to be made, bread buttered, cheese sliced, fruit added to the box ('though that almost always came back untouched).

Why would the cling film not open up? Lottie cursed as it stuck to itself, refusing to unroll in one clean sheet and being less than cooperative, tearing in bits and useless

Baker's Dozen

pieces. She'd no time to battle with this, so reached for the shiny tin foil instead. Much easier to strip off a length and much easier to cut her finger, its sharp edge doing its work, dripping blood onto the counter. A thick wad of tissue had to do, her box of plasters lying empty, as she carefully wrapped the sandwiches up and cleaned the surface next to the sink.

7.15 am. Lottie was running slightly late as she heard the beep of the washing machine, its light flashing for emphasis. She'd have to wait to hang stuff out, as Bailey the Basset needed feeding and was starting to howl an indignant protest. A bowl of dry, quality kibble was placed before the hungry hound, who enthusiastically wolfed it down, his ears swinging with every bite.

Darting upstairs to shower and dress, Lottie called for her girls to get up. The two were never early risers, happy to stay all day in bed. Averse to setting their own alarm, in the hope their mum would leave them there, Meg and Chloé ignored her cries until she appeared at their bedroom door, voice raised and waving her arms.

7.45 am and halfway through the *Today* Programme. The girls were having breakfast, lightly buttered toast and jam. Herbal tea, as they'd run out of milk, 'though neither particularly liked the taste.

8.15 am. No need for alarm, Lottie thought, backing the car out onto the drive, hooting, however, to hurry them up. Bailey was loaded into the car, for his morning walk at the local park and they all set off in a state of calm. That didn't last as the lights turned red and a queue of traffic started to form. The minutes began to tick away and before too long it was quarter to, as the dustbin lorry was up ahead.

They heard the pips at 9 am as the car finally came to a halt, decanting the girls at the school gate. Lottie watched them amble off, unconcerned at being late but looking good in their uniform, beautifully ironed and well turned out. The sense of pride that she felt was immense, as a tear trickled down her cheek.

On to the park with Bailey next, who'd fallen asleep on his usual seat. One of the advantages of getting old was that Bailey didn't want his walk and would only stop to cock his leg before clambering back inside the car, ready for his basket again.

Back at the house, they settled in. Bailey was quick to fall asleep while Lottie hauled the washing out – into the garden and up on the line, just as the heavens decided to open, letting loose torrential rain and forcing it all back in again.

9.45 am. Lottie heard the ringing of bells, coming from a room upstairs. It was then that she remembered Mother, still in bed awaiting help. Somehow, she'd just plain forgotten, in the whirl and stew of the morning rush. Up the stairs, two at a time, carrying toast and a cup of tea, still without the vital milk, Lottie having forgotten that too. The tea that spilled into the saucer Lottie used to water

Baker's Dozen

the plants, before greeting her mum with a friendly kiss in the hope she might just be forgiven. She put her mum on the commode, gave her a wash and helped her to dress, to the background sound of a phone ringing and someone leaving an urgent message.

10.30 am. Down the stairs like a woman possessed, Lottie headed to the phone, to find her appointment had been brought forward for her lump to be checked at the surgery. She glanced at the clock anxiously, as its hands, like feet, sprinted on. No time then for a cup of tea or even to sort the washing out, as Lottie shouted to her mum that she hoped she wouldn't be gone for long.

Back again within the hour, this time clutching a pint of milk, Lottie pulled the clothes horse out and quickly assembled her wet washing. On with the kettle for a much-needed drink and back up the stairs to check on her mum. The house itself seemed fast asleep, Bailey lying in his basket, Chester stretched out on the rug and her mother completely out for the count in her old, favourite, comfy chair.

Slumping down with her cup of tea, Lottie tried to gather her thoughts. She hadn't stopped the entire morning but felt she hadn't accomplished much. At least the news from the surgery was good and that was a worry off her mind.

On the dot of 12, the doorbell rang and Ted stood there with the daily post, somewhat delayed at the sorting office but ready for distribution now. Her hands going through it like flour through a sieve, most of the pile ended up in the bin. Junk mail and notices, adverts and flyers, Lottie welcomed none of it. All she had left were a couple of bills and they, of course, were less welcome still.

Flicking the door of the microwave open, she put in a quiche to warm it up. Cheese and onion, her mother's favourite. The two of them could share it for lunch. The smell of cooking awakened her pets and, there in a flash, they were at her side, waiting for any treats to fall. Lottie gave them some food of their own before taking the quiche to her mum on a tray and sat down with her for a bite and a chat.

Knowing her mum would then doze off, Lottie turned to her afternoon tasks. She'd taken a job working from home, to be fitted in as and when, four hours a day every day of the week. She knew it wasn't rocket science, stuffing envelopes, licking stamps, but it gave her a little income and made her feel needed and wanted again. She'd do some now and then some later, after collecting the girls from the local school and dropping them off at the swimming pool. The work could be monotonous but Lottie found it therapeutic as it gave her time to empty her head in this helter-skelter world of hers.

3 pm. The church bells rang unexpectedly, disturbing her semi-reverie. Then she recalled they'd just been repaired and the ringers were obviously trying them out. She loved the sound of a pealing bell as it spread out from its lofty tower, summoning worshippers to their prayer.

Baker's Dozen

She could do with divine intervention now, as her stuffing of envelopes had completely slowed down and she needed to make up the time she had lost. That, for now, would have to wait, as the girls would soon be out of school and keen to go to their swimming lesson. She'd have loved to have joined them in the pool but an hour off was out of the question and she went there and back as fast as she could.

4.15 pm. Back up the stairs to check on her mum and deliver another cup of tea, then down again to take Bailey out for a gentle walk around the block. Sniffing every blade of grass and every post he came across, Bailey wasn't one to hurry, his running days far behind him. Sometimes he'd meet Cerberus, and the two would go exploring together, seeing who had left their scent and who was new to the neighbourhood.

5 pm. Back in the car to the swimming pool, Lottie pondered the evening meal. Anything that was easy to make, that took no time and needed no fuss, but something that was still nutritious and catered for their varying tastes. She thought she'd do a Delia Smith, as Delia never got it wrong and guided you through a recipe. She'd look through her books when safely home.

5.45 pm. The girls came out with their hair still wet and eating a packet of salted crisps. Swimming gave you an appetite and dinner wasn't for ages yet. On reaching home, they raced upstairs, wet swimming gear left on the floor, their school clothes not far behind, as they quickly changed then ran to granny to tell her how their day had been.

Baker's Dozen

Lottie fed her beloved pets and poured herself a glass of wine. She deserved it after a busy day, as long as she only had the one or she'd never get up the following morning. She quickly made a Spaghetti Bolognese, 'though she knew her mum would have liked potatoes, not understanding the stringy stuff. The family of four sat down to eat, two in the dining room, two upstairs, before Lottie cleared the plates away. Dinner having been quick to consume, the girls settled down in front of the telly while Lottie attended again to her mum.

8.30 pm. Lottie glanced at the kitchen clock. She would just have time for some envelopes, to make up some of the hours she'd lost. Thirty minutes would have to do, the rest would be fitted in tomorrow, in between her other chores. At 9pm, she called it a day, rounding her daughters up for bed and checking on her lovely mum before running back down to see to her pets. A quick clean of the litter tray and waiting on Bailey in the garden before locking the door for good that night.

9.30 pm. Lottie undressed and fell into bed, exhaustion and wine totally consuming her. The pattern of days never changed and she knew she would have to do this again, minus – thank God – the doctor's surgery. She lay in her bed, unable to move, cat one side and dog the other, content that the two would be sleeping with her.

Before too long, it was 5 am and Lottie was being called again.

THE MAN WHO MARRIED THE VICAR

Matthew, it was widely agreed, was one of the handsomest men in the village. Like a young Robert Redford, he was sexy, slim, fair-haired and gorgeous. His smile was warm and his blue eyes sparkled as he charmed every woman who happened to meet him. Sadly for them, he was already taken, the vicar having snatched him up not long after her ordination. There were those who thought this a tragic waste and that the vicar should only be married to God, but the couple were so delightful together that the feelings of envy didn't last very long.

It was thought, when they first arrived in the village, that *he* was the vicar and *she* his wife, previous incumbents having always been men, until there came that Sunday in March when she'd donned her vestments and stood in the pulpit facing them. What a shock some of them had, the orthodox and traditionalists, who weren't too sure she'd ever catch on and expected her to be gone in a month.

That was twenty years ago now and the vicar and

Baker's Dozen

Matthew were not just accepted but rejoiced over in the community, raising the *te deums* to the rafters. The village had never been so well served, with the two working closely as a team and inspiring everyone they came across. Hosts of many a vicarage dinner, they took it in turns to cook the meal, and were often guests elsewhere in the village, being popular conversationalists.

The job of a vicar was very demanding and she couldn't have done it on her own. The congregation all pitched in, but it was Matthew she could never have managed without, in the day to day running of the church but even more in her personal life. She'd fallen for him as a young theologian, watching him on his motorbike, revving up and roaring off, in his faded denims and bomber jackets. She never thought she'd stand a chance but, unbeknown to her back then, Matthew had been watching her too. She had all the right qualities, those he was looking for in a wife – she was funny and caring, thoughtful and calm, but was ready for adventures of every kind and enjoyed a glass of wine or two.

Before too long, he had asked her out and the pair were often seen together, she riding pillion on his Velocette. Matthew gave up his life for her and knew, when they married, that he'd play second fiddle as his wife's vocation would always come first. Not that he minded that at all, for Matthew adored his godly wife who, in her turn, idolised him, putting him high on a pedestal.

Baker's Dozen

Always a Matthew, never a Matt, his name itself meant "gift of God" and that, in a way, was how she saw him, as the greatest gift she could ever have been given. It also amused her that, in the Bible, the apostle Matthew was known as Levi, which reminded her of his denim jeans. The apostle, however, travelled on foot, not on a 60s motorbike, but that just made the vicar laugh.

Matthew quickly learnt the ropes and threw himself into parish work, regularly seen out and about and serving the local community. A lot of the jobs he did himself, knuckling down from the word go, a practical and an able man who enjoyed working, both indoors and out.

The vicar asked him to start a choir and get the village singing again. That, for Matthew, was easy to do, as he came from a very musical family. His mum played the organ in her local church while his dad conducted in the Philharmonic. Matthew himself liked to sing and played a number of instruments, from piano and harp to guitar and flute. He seemed to have a natural talent and was happy to put it to good use. It was also a way to get to know people and for them, in turn, to meet each other, in a friendly and easy-going setting.

It didn't take long for the choir to be formed, with the highest vocal range to the lowest: soprano, alto, tenor and bass. Matthew arranged the music himself and the choir rehearsed once a week, members bringing their instruments along, if the hymns were to be accompanied. More often

Baker's Dozen

than not, they sang *a cappella* and sometimes with just a soloist. On occasion, that would be Cerberus, who came with Bob to the Sunday service and would like to howl unannounced. Nobody ever seemed to mind and the vicar was pleased that the dog joined in. All were welcome in the vicar's church.

Once the choir was up and running, Matthew turned to the church bells. They hadn't been rung for quite some time, the older ringers having passed away and no one new having ventured forth. Certain that this could be rectified, Matthew began a recruitment campaign. Soon enough, a band was formed and, after some months of discordant ringing, the bells once again were harmonious, as the ringers began to improve their skills, practising every Thursday night under the guidance of their ringing master – also known as Ted the postman, who'd been a ringer all his life.

The vicar received some complaints at first, largely from Ken and his wife Darlene, neither being church-going types and rejoicing in something new to criticise. But their sneering didn't last too long as they witnessed a new social group and one that appeared to be having fun. It kept them active in various ways – physically, mentally and socially, as they burned calories and toned muscles and strove to remember the sequences. The sound of the bells in itself was calming, to those who were ringing and those who heard them, as they pealed out in the late summer sun.

Baker's Dozen

The bells were rung on various occasions, as the village was accompanied in its joy and its grief – a cheerful ring for the latest wedding, a sad, slow toll that announced a death. Like the sombre knell for Gabriella that rang out from the tower of the church as the funeral cortège made its way, sadly and slowly through the lychgate, stopping briefly at the coffin rest before continuing its journey down the path.

The churchyard was kept in immaculate condition by Matthew and some of the villagers. Knowing it to be a sacred place, they all felt it their spiritual duty to keep it tidy and in a good state. Some of the graves were very old but Matthew tended each with care, ensuring that no one was ever forgotten. The vicar had asked him to update the list that detailed all who were buried there – no small or easy task, that kept him busy for years on end. The records kept had been far from complete, but Matthew worked diligently, gathering data from every source and piecing together a number of stories.

He liked to wander in the churchyard alone, drawn by its beauty, history and peace, praying for those who were buried there and marvelling at the variety of stones, each telling its own tale and each with its own decorative feature, be it angels, lambs, wheat or urns, setting off his imagination. There was only so much that a stone could tell, by the name engraved, family and age, but Matthew tried to fill in the gaps, seeing these sleepers as real people, as such they all once were. Some were still visited but most

Baker's Dozen

were not, except by Matthew and his team of labourers who cleaned the stones and mended the kerbs, removed the weeds and cut the grass.

Inside the church was another team (mostly women), arranging flowers and cleaning the brasses, dusting the pews and scrubbing the floors. The backbone of the church community, it would all have fallen apart without them, as the vicar and Matthew knew only too well. They were lucky to have a church at all, as many had now been deconsecrated, turned into flats or a liquor mart. Having stood on this site for 900 years, St Luke's, Little Bunting, could hang out its flags with the vicar and Matthew waving them. They knew that the church had to adapt, to continue to serve the community, and they regularly held events in the hall, from Sunday lunches to reading groups, Zumba classes and keep fit.

St Luke, they were sure, would approve of all this, as he gazed down upon them from his stained-glass window. The church looked beautiful as the sunlight came through, the colours from the glass peacefully lying on the stone paving, like the patterns in a kaleidoscope. Matthew would often sit at night, in a peaceful church, alone in a pew, mesmerised by its quiet beauty. He thought of those who had worshipped there, of the milestones in a person's life, to which the church had borne witness – the hatchings, matchings and despatchings, as his wife liked to call them.

Each would appear in the newsletter, which Matthew

Baker's Dozen

drafted for the vicar's approval. She, in turn, would draft her sermon and read it aloud for her husband to comment, especially if likely to hit a nerve. Better fall foul of an audience of one than upset an entire congregation. The numbers had doubled since the vicar first came and she wasn't going to jeopardise that.

Whenever they could, they would hold a soirée, back home in the vicarage, an all-inclusive get together, with good conversation and merriment. The vicar and Matthew liked to dance, so music often ended the meal, and the two would take the floor together, encouraging others to do the same.

But midweek nights were sacrosanct and, barring disaster, saved for each other. When possible, they'd go out for the day, walking in the country lanes or taking off on the motorbike. They'd take some food and sit by the stream, enjoying each other's company, then home again for afternoon tea and some of Andrew's gingerbread men. He teased them with the figures he made, piping on icing to look like clothes, in the shape – he thought – of the villagers. Every time they opened the tin, they tried to guess who the characters were, laughed when they saw themselves depicted and marvelled at Andrew's consummate skill. If only the vicar could see him wed, and not just to his bakery. But to Matthew she had to acquiesce when he told her not to interfere. She knew he was right, as he often was, but she would have liked it all the same. Matthew smiled at his adoring wife, who he knew had been truly heaven sent. In truth, he cared little who she tried to marry, for the best in the world was wedded to him.

UNQUIET SLUMBERS

The house had been said to be haunted for as long as anyone could remember. As a little girl, Ginny had always run past it, fearful of what she might see. She'd never actually seen anything, but she always thought that she might and the idea of it hastened her on. Whenever she could, she'd avoid it, go round the other way, but sometimes she had to go past and then she ran like the wind. Heart pounding, head swirling, Ginny bolted home, terror clipping her heels, fear seizing her mind.

Her mother had tried to calm her, had tried to laugh it off; there was nobody there to hurt her and the dead wouldn't cause any harm. Yet she thought herself it was haunted and had heard all the terrible tales. Better not to go near it and to leave it to itself. She'd tuck Ginny up in bed each night and wait till she'd gone to sleep, but Ginny would wake at the slightest sound and scream the neighbourhood down.

Thirty years on, she was no less scared, as she approached the house again. There it stood, as it always had, at the end of the lane by the stream. Its walls dark and dreary, its frontage cold and forbidding, it still looked grim

Baker's Dozen

and unfriendly, cheerless and uninviting. It weighted itself to the ground, solid, heavy and cumbersome, suggesting a long permanence and a hardened state of being.

Nobody lived there now and the house was derelict, giving off a solemn sadness and a sombre, unloved air. No birds sang in the woods, no fish swam in the stream, nobody walked down its moss-covered path and no light entered there.

Entrenched in its landscape, the old house stood, its windows, like eyes, watching out, waiting for any passers-by to linger by the gate. As Ginny stood, pinned to the ground, she shivered in this unearthly spot, wondering whether to carry on or go back round the longer way. The brooding house could still unnerve her, reach into her very soul, disturb her just by being there, challenge her to meet its stare.

The path through the gate was overgrown, covered in weeds and fallen branches. Ivy crawled along the edges, its tendrils seeming to beckon her on. Something in her couldn't resist and she flipped the latch on the rusty gate.

She slid now and then on the wet moss as she inched her way along the path, trying not to slip right over, leaving herself exposed and open. The gabled house rose up before her, declaring its overwhelming strength as it stretched up to its full height, making her cower and shrink before it, like an animal frightened by a predator.

She sensed that someone was watching her, as her eyes

traced over the dirty windows, scanning for any sign of movement. But nothing stirred in that quiet house, nothing to tear the silence apart.

Ginny turned and retraced her steps, all the while looking over her shoulder, conscious that someone else was there, some unseen spirit or fallen angel, intent on spite and malevolence.

She made her way back through the village and stopped at the café close to the church. Kathleen and Thelma were taking tea, together with Jean, the postman's wife. The three women were deeply engrossed and barely noticed when Ginny came in. Sitting down at a table nearby, she ordered a cup of tea and a scone and looked about the little room. The café hadn't existed before, when Ginny lived here as a girl, but seemed to be a welcome retreat, pleasant, orderly, pretty and clean.

As she sat quietly sipping her tea and mulling over the disused house, the voices of the women carried and penetrated Ginny's ear. She couldn't help but hear one tell of strange goings-on up at the house, not just in the distant past but recent and often and menacing. Ginny inclined her head to hear, trying not to be obtrusive while straining to catch the women's words, their faces betraying the shock of it all.

At last, she approached the women direct and said she had overheard them speak and wanted to introduce herself. She'd lived in the village until she was ten, when her family had moved to Derbyshire. Most of her life had been there since, until the offer of a job in a nearby town had attracted her back to her childhood village. Currently staying at a B&B, she was looking out for a new home before starting her post in three months' time. As the senior historian and archivist, Ginny would be carrying out some research, her first work to be on the haunted house.

The women looked from one to another, furrows creasing, rendered speechless. Shifting uncomfortably in her chair, Kathleen was the first to speak, advising Ginny to think better of it and not to visit the house again. A woman had been seen at night, walking through the woods alone, drifting over the fallen leaves, her feet hovering above the ground. Dressed as one from a bygone age, hooded and in a long, white robe, she disappeared amongst the trees, later to emerge in front of the house. Passing through the green front door, she cast an eerie light about her, slowly moving from room to room, until darkness shrouded the house again.

This had not been the only sighting and not the only strange occurrence. Ted had seen an open window while cutting through on his daily round. As he walked the lane beside the house, the smell of baking wafted out, and a woman in a cloak and veil turned and looked directly at him. Footsteps were heard upon the lane and, sensing he was not alone, Ted broke into a gentle run, his pursuer seeming to gain on him. He didn't stop till he reached his

Baker's Dozen

house, breathless and without his bag. The post all scattered on the lane, he'd later gone to pick it up, finding however that none was there, his bag lying empty on the ground.

Jean remembered his face that day, white and in a state of shock. He couldn't speak for half an hour, his eyes bulged and he didn't blink. He only stared in front of him as if possessed or paralysed. She'd gone with him to collect his post, later, in the afternoon but, save for the empty messenger bag, nothing appeared to be untoward.

Ginny listened to the mysterious tales, completely absorbed by what she heard. She told them of her own experience and how she felt as a little girl. Jean vaguely remembered her, as she'd lived in the village for so long and had always known of the abandoned house. She thought she remembered Ginny's mother, 'though it was all such a long time ago now. She suggested she talk to Andrew Baker as he had another story to tell, from when he'd first arrived in the village and, again, of a recent happening.

Ginny met Andrew the following day, after his morning delivery round. He seemed reluctant to talk at first, as he wasn't sure where this would lead and was trying his very best to forget. At length, however, he opened up, over a coffee and a slice of cake, accompanied by his friend, the vicar.

He told of the day he'd arrived at the house, clutching a bag of white, soft rolls, ordered by someone the previous night. A simple note had been left at his door, requesting he

Baker's Dozen

bring the rolls to the house at half-past nine the following day. Andrew had never been there before and hadn't heard of its reputation, so set off happy and unsuspecting. Whistling to himself as he unlocked the gate, he carried on up the path, thinking how it needed some love and – truth to tell – a lot of work.

The house before him was very imposing and looked like it hadn't received much attention. Someone had lit a fire that day, as smoke billowed out from a central chimney, the other two – at each end of the house – damaged and crumbling and in need of repair. As he approached, he sensed some movement, 'though not a soul was there to be seen. He looked around, as he heard a noise, a rustling in the undergrowth, but saw no sign of man or beast and thought his mind must be playing tricks.

The bell-pull, at the side of the porch, was worn and old-fashioned and didn't ring, so Andrew knocked upon the door, waiting to see who would welcome him. He knocked again, after waiting a while, and when no one came to answer him, he placed the rolls on an alcove shelf, in the dry and under cover. He stood in the porch, looking about him, wondering where the inhabitants were. He glanced back down to the rolls he had placed, but to his surprise, there was nothing there. Nobody had come to the door and nobody had come before him. They hadn't fallen on the floor; they'd simply vanished, without trace.

Andrew started to feel unnerved, knowing that he had

Baker's Dozen

put them there. He felt a hand run through his hair and tried at first to shake it off, thinking it must be just a breeze, but the air was still and nothing moved and there was nobody there in the porch but him.

Walking quickly down the path, it seemed like the trees were closing in. Clouds were gathering overhead and drops of rain were starting to fall. Darkness had fallen all around him, 'though it was only just a quarter to ten. On reaching the village, he'd met the vicar, who found him in a dreadful state, trembling and nervous and ill at ease. She took him home and calmed him down, 'though her heart and mind were sorely troubled. She'd heard the stories about the house but had never herself ventured there. It seemed that it was not at peace, unable to rest and agitated.

Ginny listened to Andrew's tale, the vicar sitting at his side. Something unnatural was happening here, as she knew too well from yesterday and from years ago as a little child. The worry now was her piece of research and how she would ever accomplish it, if she was frightened to go to the house itself.

The vicar then told her own tale, following on from Andrew's fright. She'd gone on her own, within a week, to see what all the fuss was about, believing herself in the hands of God. She'd always been a sensible woman, not given to fear or imaginings, and had set off in an emotionless way, with an open mind and a steady heart.

The house, she thought, looked mournful and sad,

Baker's Dozen

neglected and full of emptiness as if it were crying out for love. She stood at the gate and looked down the path, at the stream that ran by the side of it. Nothing stirred as she paused for a moment, no light came through the canopy of trees, not a single bird was flitting about. All was still, all was quiet.

Seconds later, as she looked at the house, the door opened and a woman came out. She stood on the step with a lighted taper, strange considering the time of day, and seemed to beckon the vicar on. Through the gate and down the path, the vicar walked with easy steps, till something stopped her in her tracks. The woman was dressed in clerical clothes, in black array with a white dog collar. More remarkable was the woman's face – identical to the vicar herself. It was as if she was looking in a mirror, her movements copied by the figure in front. Every time she moved her head, her doppelgänger did the same. They stood there, smiling at each other, the vicar thinking it some kind of trick and half expecting the prankster to jump out or for an elaborate gadget to be revealed. No such thing occurred, however, and the figure just kept walking on, till it passed straight through her and disappeared.

The vicar looked round at an empty space, puzzled at where the woman had gone. She carried on to the house itself, undeterred but on her guard. The door was closed and the curtains drawn, 'though she swore they'd been open a moment ago. She knocked but nobody answered her call. As she turned and walked back down the path, she heard the sound of distant voices, like a choir singing an ancient lament. She saw through the trees a little cortège that faded away as she looked at it.

Something surreal was happening here, unless of course it *was* a joke and someone out to scare them all. The house had been empty for quite some time but who were these figures that kept coming back, restless, unsettled, unable to sleep? Something else was troubling the vicar: the image of herself she'd seen, quite uncanny, there before her, till disappearing through her body. It hadn't hurt or caused her harm but she knew of the legend that always said that, if you chanced to see your own double, your death would occur within the year. Superstitious nonsense perhaps, but a niggling worry all the same.

Sitting in the café now, with Andrew and Ginny at her side, it all seemed as part of a dream or something she had read in a book, but too many sightings quashed that thought and Andrew began his final tale.

It happened only days ago, when he took Cerberus out for a walk. The little dog was off his lead and, before Andrew could stop him going, he'd run down the lane at the side of the house. Having no choice but to follow him, Andrew reluctantly went in pursuit. This time, as he neared the house, he heard a gentle, rhythmic rumble and a creaking of wooden machinery. The dog, having sensed whence it came, had taken off round the back of the house, Andrew

Baker's Dozen

then trailing in his wake. As he turned the corner, he saw the dog, fixed rigid upon the spot, fur standing up all over his body, then letting out an almighty howl. Andrew ran at speed to his side and picked him up to comfort him.

In front of them both, a number of men, busying about, back and forth. All were dressed in old aprons and smocks with a simple cap upon their heads, covered in layers of flour dust. It was like watching a movie reel, only this was enacted without a screen and played out there in front of them. One of the men caught Andrew's eye and looked at him from another world, as if seeing his own future there, with Andrew in turn a witness to his past. At the sound of a bell, the men disappeared and Andrew and Cerberus were all alone. A sense of peace came over them now, as they wended their way back down the lane, crossing the bridge over the stream and into their own reality.

Ginny knew not what to make of it all, as she pondered the stories she'd just been told. Before too long, she would start her research and hopefully get to the bottom of it.

Six months later and in her new home – a cosy cottage in Little Bunting – Ginny was holding a dinner party. Her guests were those she'd previously met when she'd come to stay at the B&B. When the meal was over, they settled down, with coffee and liqueurs, in the comfy chairs, her research on the house to be revealed.

It had started life as a manor house, with rich pasture and arable land, back in the early 1800s. Outbuildings had once existed, including a cowshed, stables and coach-house, at one stage all in excellent use. As the cost of running the estate grew, and its lord and lady passed away, the manor began to deteriorate. Their daughter had become a nun, in the mendicant order of the Carmelites and, when she died, she bequeathed the manor, there being no other direct descendants. The coach-house became a tiny chapel, the manor itself home to the nuns, who tended the land and lived there peacefully, till one by one their God called them home.

For a number of years, the house was deserted, falling further into decay, till a young businessman bought it up and turned it into a flour mill. The outbuildings were all converted and it became a small but thriving operation with a single grade of finished flour. In time, the owner himself had died and the house began its steady decline, the outbuildings crumbling one by one, their ruins becoming an eerie presence.

To the friends gathered at Ginny's table, the history of the house made perfect sense, chiming well with the figures they'd seen and the unsettling scenes they had witnessed there. But the house itself was not at peace, its spirits wandering unquiet still.

For Andrew, there was more to come when Ginny revealed its inhabitants, the fruits of her labours and fine research. The lord of the manor, by a quirk of fate, bore the name – like Andrew – of Baker. Although the two were

Baker's Dozen

not related, it seemed to Andrew a trifle spooky when he thought of the hand upon his head. A further twist was the mill itself, with all the flour and bread it produced. The owner of the mill, the businessman, was born a Scot and called Andrew, adding another kink to the tale.

It somehow seemed it was meant to be, that Andrew had come to Little Bunting and set up his own bakery. His friends now thought he should buy the house and turn it back into a mill. Perhaps, in time, it would find its peace, when loved, cherished and restored again. Andrew liked the thought himself, despite its macabre goings-on and all the anguish it had often caused. He saw the house in a different light and felt he might be happy there. But within a year, the vicar had died and the stories started up again.

Vida Cody was born and grew up in south east London. She graduated from the University of Southampton with a degree in Spanish and went on to gain a Masters in Hispanic Studies from the University of London. She has lived and worked in Spain and Peru and has travelled widely for both pleasure and business. Introduced to books at a very early age, Vida has had a strong love of literature ever since. *Baker's Dozen* is her second collection of stories.